Friends, Russians, and Countrymen

FRIENDS, RUSSIANS, AND COUNTRYMEN

A NOVEL

Hampton Howard

ST. MARTIN'S PRESS
NEW YORK

The quotation on page 183, from "Coming" in *The Less Deceived* by Philip Larkin, is reprinted by permission of the Marvell Press, London, U.K.

FRIENDS, RUSSIANS, AND COUNTRYMEN. Copyright © 1988 by Hampton Howard. All rights reserved. Printed in the United States of America. No part of this book may be used or reproduced in any manner whatsoever without written permission except in the case of brief quotations embodied in critical articles or reviews. For information, address St. Martin's Press, 175 Fifth Avenue, New York, N.Y. 10010.

Design by Claire Counihan

Library of Congress Cataloging-in-Publication Data

Howard, Hampton.
    Friends, Russians, and countrymen / by Hampton Howard.
        p.   cm.
    ISBN 0-312-01432-5 : $16.95
        I. Title.
PS3558.08817F7 1988
813'.54—dc19   87-27481

First Edition
10 9 8 7 6 5 4 3 2 1

For Lady, as always,
and for
Robert Emmett Ginna, Jr.,
with gratitude for his advice,
encouragement, and wholly
gratuitous kindness.

FRIENDS, RUSSIANS, AND COUNTRYMEN

CHAPTER ONE

THE possibility of the existence of a penetration agent at the Arms Control and Disarmament Agency first entered the bureaucratic record in the form of the handwritten minutes of a meeting held on the 28th of March at the National Security Agency complex at Fort Meade, Maryland.

The meeting was held on the second floor of the Operations Building, and was attended only by a senior NSA signals analyst, a junior archivist from the NSA's Sensitive Materials Center, who served as stenographer, the director of security for the State Department Bureau of Intelligence and Research, and the deputy director of operations of the Central Intelligence Agency.

It was 11:15 A.M. when the color-coded doors of the conference room opened and the visitors from INR and CIA emerged, accompanied by the junior archivist who was their nominal sponsor. Leaving the nervous young clerk at the head of the escalator, the two men descended to C corridor and entered the pedestrian traffic, passing branch offices of Equitable Trust, Tower Federal Credit Union, and Ticketron before the INR man, whose name was Reynolds, spoke. Reynolds was short, round, and unimposing, and affected a compensatory gruffness of tone.

"So you tell me, Mr. Blaine," he said, addressing the younger man and using the pronouns like clubs, from habit, "what do you think?"

Blaine, the deputy director of operations, was very nearly Reynold's physical opposite. Tall, thin, graceless, and boyish, he had in youth judged as useful, and thus adopted, the style of dress and carriage inculcated by his Episcopal preparatory school; a judgment which, in the thirty intervening years, he had found no reason to revise.

"To be perfectly candid, Mac," he said, "it's a bit thin. What have we got? One anomalous article in a Soviet military journal and an incomplete fragment of a nine-month-old SIGINT intercept. Not exactly the sort of evidence that a competent prosecutor would care to take to court."

"I suppose not," Reynolds said, "but then, if that sort of evidence existed, it'd be the Bureau I'd have to be talking to today instead of you. You told me, you said we ever get something like this, that what you wanted was a head start. That's what this is. No guarantees at all."

"Don't misunderstand me," Blaine said, as the men turned into the glass-enclosed hallway leading from the Operations Building to Headquarters Tower. "We're very grateful. If you have any problems with the Bureau on this just give me a call."

"There aren't going to *be* any problems with the Bureau," Reynolds said firmly. "Far's I'm concerned, this's just one more conversation we never had, and twenty-four hours from now, tops, the Bureau'll have everything that you do. I don't have any choice about that."

"I understand perfectly, Mac," Blaine said. "That's why I had Bullard put me on the NSC agenda for this afternoon."

"Anything else an old alum can do for his alma mater?" Reynolds asked.

"As a matter of fact," Blaine said, slowing but not stopping,

2

"there is. You said that Butterfield first noticed the article on Monday night while he was reading in his office. Does that mean he keeps the journals there?"

"Yup," Reynolds said. "Stacks of 'em, all over the place."

"And he sees the gentleman in question every day, I suppose, as a matter of normal business?"

"I imagine so," Reynolds said. "Except maybe when one or the other of them's in Washington."

"Then let's do this," Blaine said. "Have Butterfield call the fellow into his office and show him the article. As if he'd just read it. 'Hey! Look at this! Could this just be coincidence, or do you think we should talk to the security people?' That sort of thing. Have him make it very clear that he hasn't broached the subject elsewhere. It might be interesting to see what he does."

"When would you want Butterfield to do this?" Reynolds asked.

"Right away," Blaine said without hesitation. "Early next week. Before the Bureau has a chance to get its oar in. Any problem with that?"

"Not with that," Reynolds said, as they signed out with the FPS guards and surrendered their one-day passes, "but I *do* have a question."

"Go ahead," Blaine said. "You've got one coming."

"When I called with this," Reynolds said, shrugging on his coat and not meeting Blaine's eyes, "I talked to Bullard and everything, and I was just wondering, if this guy turns out to be a live one, like I think he's going to, well, who gets it? Whose operation is this going to be? You can tell me that it's none of my business and I'll understand. I'm just curious, is all."

Together the two men passed through the doors of Gatehouse 1 and descended the steps to the rotary drive and visitors' carpark beyond. At the base of the steps Blaine stopped and turned to Reynolds.

"Stuarti," he said.

"*Paris* Stuarti?" Reynolds asked, raising his eyebrows.

"Yes," Blaine said, unsmiling. "Do you know him?"

"No," Reynolds said. "I know *of* him, though. The guy must be a hundred, for Christ's sake."

"Well, he's not," Blaine said. "Stuarti's one of those people who probably looked about seventy when he was thirty. Now that he *is* seventy, he understandably looks a bit older."

"I heard he can't even *walk*," Reynolds said.

"Well," said Blaine, somewhat more tersely, "if footspeed were a primary concern I suppose I'd have to give some consideration to a younger man. But it's not. Stuarti is smart and *very* experienced. Plus he's a forger, and a con artist, which is what we need, and he knows all the right people. It's how he supplements his income as a civil servant."

"It'd seem like *you* know all the right people," Reynolds observed. "I mean, you can pick up the phone in your car and talk to the president."

"That's not the sort of people I was talking about," Blaine said softly.

"I also understand that the guy's a little *weird*," Reynolds said, beginning to smile despite himself.

"That's just Bullard whining," Blaine said. "Stuarti always bullies him. Still, I suppose it's possible that an unbiased observer might give you the 'weird.' "

As the two men stood talking at the bottom of the steps, a black Chrysler Newport driven by a hard-faced young man glided to the curb and waited, idling. There was a large splash of fresh bird droppings on the passenger's side of the windshield.

"You think this is what people mean when they talk about life outside the Beltway?" Reynolds asked, pointing to the droppings.

"Must be," Blaine said, opening the passenger door. "Nature red in tooth and claw, Mac. I'd like you to check in every six hours until Bullard tells you we're on him."

"No problem," Reynolds said, as Blaine entered the car and closed the door behind him.

Slowly the car slid from the curb and passed without stopping through the double gates in the cyclone fencing. The day was brilliant, and as the car turned right on Savage Road, heading for the Baltimore-Washington Parkway, the shadows cast by the enormous radomes atop the tan, nine-story Headquarters Tower swept briefly across it, like those of silent carrion birds.

CHAPTER TWO

THE telephone repairman wore no bra, and beneath a thin T-shirt bearing the legend NUKE THE WHALES her nipples protruded, as Mrs. Porter confided with tipsy courage to the Butterfields that evening over her special salmon mousse, well, dear, like *thumbs.* Not at *all,* she added, what one expected to find at one's door in Greenwich, Connecticut.

"I didn't bother with a bra in my first ten K," Joy Butterfield said grimly, "and by the time I hit the tape my nipples were *bleeding.*"

Joy was a bustless and cadaverous woman of fifty who had, ten months prior, abandoned a decade of analysis in favor of aerobic fitness. While salutary for her corollary circulation, the change of focus had proven disastrous for her conversation, and in recent months the weekly dinner that the Porters and Butterfields had shared since Dr. Butterfield's transfer to the New York area—the men had been college roommates—had gradually become for Mrs. Porter an occasion of dull dread.

"Plus," Mrs. Porter continued bravely, "with her boots, and her helmet, and her tool belt slung around her hips, she looked just like a *gunslinger . . .*"

6

"Repaired phones like a gunslinger, too," said Mr. Porter. "This morning we had three phones that worked, now we've only got the one in the study."

"Not just chafed," Joy added severely, "*cracked.*"

"My *dear*," Mrs. Porter said with as much solicitousness as she could muster, "whatever did you *do*?"

"Rice," answered Dr. Walter Butterfield, a portly research mathematician who loathed exercise in its every form.

"Rice?" Mrs. Porter said helplessly.

"*R*est, *i*ce, *c*ompression, and *e*levation," Dr. Butterfield explained, lavishly buttering a roll. "It's what she does when she's not running, though given Joy's age and temperament I'd have to see the elevation part to believe it."

"Laugh all you like, El Gordo," Joy snarled, "just keep your policies up to date."

Dr. Butterfield popped the entire roll into his mouth, waggled his eyebrows like Groucho Marx at his wife, and turned again to his conversation with Mr. Porter, his face filled with bread and collegial affinity.

"The reason he's so smug tonight," Joy whispered savagely, turning her back on the men, "is that I've been forced to give up LSD."

"*What?*"

"Bad for the knees."

"*What?*"

"That's *l*ong *s*low *d*istance, Louise," said Joy, unsmiling, "not the drug."

Mrs. Porter shuddered and again filled her glass, abominating acronyms and Joy's compulsions. "I'm sure you'll find something else, dear."

"I have," Joy whispered, leaning closer.

"That's nice . . ."

"*Fartlek!*"

Mrs. Porter, unfamiliar with the lexicon of runners, slumped visibly in her chair, like an animal taking a bullet. "Pardon me?" she whimpered.

Brutally, Joy repeated the dreadful word, her eyes alight with zealot fire.

No reply, of course, was possible, so the sudden peal of the telephone in the study seemed to Mrs. Porter, in her torment, a direct and merciful intervention by the Angel of Providence.

No one, after all, secure in the warmth of friendship and plenty, had reason to suspect that it might be the Other Angel.

The library of the Porters' home was an elegant room, richly decorated in books, leather, and Federal period furniture. As Dr. Butterfield, finger-combing crumbs from his mustache, entered the room in response to his hostess's summons he remarked with anticipation the evening's dessert— an almond torte flanked by two bottles of chilled Sauternes —which sat on the room's sideboard.

The call to Dr. Butterfield was brief.

The first sound that he heard on identifying himself was a thinly fluted A-flat, produced, he guessed with some puzzlement, on an ordinary choirmaster's pitchpipe.

The last sound that he heard was a clear middle C, which, while effectively saving him from the torte's temptation, irrecoverably spoiled the dessert course for the others, activating as it did an acoustic detonating pencil that in turn fired the C4 explosive with which the handset had been packed.

The material of Dr. Butterfield's head, varying as head material does in density, did not therefore blow neatly away in strict accordance with the laws of ballistics, but rather distributed itself about the room with appalling randomness. Indeed, hours of painstaking labor were later required by the responding pathologist before he was able with certainty to identify the pink lump on the Seymour mahogany heartback side chair as a portion of ear, zygomatic and mastoid bones, to point out the two molars and coronoid process of the mandible between the antique glass cake stand and the Wedgwood majolica serving plates, and to hypothesize as vitreous

8

humor the liquid glazing both the untouched torte and the sideboard on which it still sat (Hepplewhite, mahogany, veneered doors of cherry and mixed woods).

In a squalid studio apartment on Ninth Street east of Avenue B, forty-five minutes and half a million dollars away from the Porters' Greenwich home, a dark-haired young woman wearing white bikini underpants and a T-shirt reading NUKE THE WHALES sat cross-legged on an unmade bed, a telephone receiver in one hand and an ordinary choirmaster's pitchpipe in the other. For a moment she listened with seeming puzzlement to the dial tone that the phone emitted, then hung up and replaced both phone and pitchpipe on a low coffee table next to the bed.

"I'm not sure," she said, addressing her guest and frowning becomingly to underscore her concern. "It just cut off and all I got was a dial tone."

The man to whom she spoke was thickset and flaxen-haired, and as she spoke he rose from the chair where he had been watching her and crossed to the room's single window.

"That is all right," he said, in an accent that might have been north German. "That is perfectly normal." Unhurriedly he locked the window and lowered the shade.

"Good," the girl said thickly, stirred both by her success and his preparations. "Let me do the machine."

Standing, she stretched langorously and stepped to the table at the end of the bed, on which sat an automatic answering machine. Depressing a button, she began to reach for the machine's microphone before the man's voice, as he turned from the window, stopped her.

"A dial tone is all right," he said quietly, his "s" hissing slightly and "all right" pronounced as a single word. "It is a click or series of clicks that indicates a faulty circuit."

"You're the one who should know," she said deferentially, thinking again of the undeniably impressive credentials that he had only the past evening shown her in strictest confidence.

"And there weren't any clicks at all, so I guess the bug's working."

Flashing an inviting smile over her shoulder, the girl turned again to the machine.

As she did so, her guest's thick arm slid easily over her shoulder, curling around her throat and jerking her backward against him. Her larynx crushed and her vision swimming, she never saw the short razor-edged linoleum knife which he then drove into the top of her abdomen just beneath the intercostal arch and with a single, effortless motion drew down to her pubis, the blade passing through muscle and integument with the same ease, and much the same soft tearing sound, as it would have through fabric.

Lowering the eviscerated girl lightly to the floor, her visitor removed from his coat a folded shopping bag from the Pottery Barn. In this he placed the linoleum knife, the pitchpipe, and from the room's single table a yellow hard hat lettered Southern New England Telephone. He did not look at her as he left, turning off the light and closing the door softly behind him.

In the darkened room, shadowed only by the dim light from a single window giving onto an airshaft, the dark-haired girl sat propped against the wall, cradling her intestines in her arms like a child.

In a cracked whisper, the only sound that she could make, she spoke three times, calling first on her mother for aid, then on her God for absolution, and finally, perhaps suspecting the one to be golfing and the other dead, saying, or so it sounded, "Oh! Lookit, Grandma!" before her features settled abruptly into the surprise of death, tipping the room into a silence broken only by the almost inaudible hissing of the answering machine's recorder, a noise so soft that even her visitor had failed to remark it.

In all, it took her three minutes to die, and it must be considered less an ironic anomaly than a testament to the resilience of youth and the sophistication of modern communications that the confirmation of her death reached a small group of very concerned senior functionaries in Moscow's Dzerzhinsky Square (where it was then 4:42 in the morning) a full forty seconds before it actually occurred.

Within an hour of the explosion the major New York newspapers received by messenger identical copies of a manifesto signed by an organization calling itself the Fifteenth of June Group claiming credit for the assassination, not of Dr. Butterfield, but of Mr. Porter, whom the Group characterized as "a running dog of scientific imperialism" whose extermination was merely the logical manifestation of a vigilant and outraged "people's justice."

The newspapers made much of the incident.

The simple fact of terrorism, even botched terrorism, in Greenwich, Connecticut, (for who now was safe?) and the appalling photos (obtained by the *New York Post* for an astronomical sum and published over the caption "Reach Out and Touch Someone") dominated the front pages. The editorial pages spoke bitingly of the moral and juridical difference between justice and murder, and decried the loss of "innocent" life inevitable in the confusion of the two, distinctions that poor Mr. Porter, an investment banker whose single and tenuous connection with science was a seat on Union Carbide's board, found disquieting in their implication.

Of the late Dr. Butterfield little was said, perhaps because the purely fortuitous nature of his death rendered him a subsidiary rather than central character in the drama, and more probably because a continued and churlish refusal by the family to grant interviews or to weep on television leached the "innocent bystander" angle of much of its emotional punch.

The newspapers thus variously referred to him as "an intimate friend of the intended victim," "a distinguished scientist," and "a loving husband and father whose pointless death must be considered the stuff of tragedy."

11

Indeed, only *The New York Times*, to whom credentials matter perhaps overmuch, thought it necessary to note that at the time of his death Dr. Butterfield had been employed as a senior civilian consultant to the Arms Control and Disarmament Agency.

CHAPTER THREE

THE small interrogation room at the FBI field office on Centre Street was institutional green, smelled vaguely of vomit and Lysol, and contained only a single Formica-topped table and three sideless wooden chairs.

Thirty years of experience with such chairs had taught Senior Special Agent Francis Minihan the futility of trying to find a comfortable position, and thus he did not bother to try but merely sat watching sourly as Edward Stuarti, straightening slightly in his wheelchair and holding a paper napkin closely beneath his chin, bit deeply into a jelly doughnut.

"They told me you'd been sick," Minihan said severely, "but this is even more depressing than I figured it'd be. You look godawful."

Slumped in the wheelchair, Stuarti indeed looked like a composed study in illness and eccentricity. He wore an overlarge black velveteen suit derived, if not dated, from the *fin de siècle*. A lined cape fastened at the throat was wrapped about his shoulders, a lap blanket covered his legs, and a blue beret, pulled down squarely and aggressively on his head, forced his ears out sharply to either side. His face was pallid with fatigue, for he had slept little in the past forty-eight hours and was unaccustomed to jet travel.

"I've always said that the Bureau was a class act, Frank," Stuarti replied, his mouth full. "You could've just gotten a couple of glazed or something, you didn't need to get the jelly. But you did, and I appreciate it."

"You owe me a buck forty-five," Minihan said.

" 'Artificial dairy product'?" Stuarti read, holding the small white pleated container close to his better eye. "What the hell's that?"

"Your skin's all gray, for Christ's sake," Minihan said. "What've you been *doing*?"

"Serving my country in Switzerland, Frank," Stuarti said gravely. "Where it rained for six straight weeks."

"Doing what?" Minihan demanded.

"Making friends with a couple of Swiss guards," Stuarti said, taking another bite.

"You're shitting me," Minihan said incredulously. "Am I going to wake up one of these mornings and find some banner headline in *The Times* reading, 'Swiss Guards Cross Tiber; Vatican Cites Need for Defensible Borders'?"

"Not *those* Swiss guards, Frank," Stuarti said. "I'm talking about a couple of cantonal constables. The Red Cross has been interning Soviet officers captured in Afghanistan in Switzerland. Turns out there was a GRU signals lieutenant somebody thought we should talk to. I had to make friends with the local guards first."

"Did the guy want to talk?"

"More'n he wanted to *live*," Stuarti said. "They'd had him on a farm in Ticino for six months and the poor guy was on his knees with terminal boredom and homesickness. Couldn't stop moaning. 'Rain, cows, banks, litter baskets . . .' When I showed up with a chessboard and some vodka I must have looked like the Angel Gabriel."

"Angel Gabriel, my hump," said Minihan, whose short

14

white hair was as carefully barbered as Stuarti's long gray hair was not. "You look like an old faggot."

"Give me a break, Frank," Stuarti said, dumping the creamer into his coffee, "I *am* an old faggot. Not to hurt your feelings or anything, but you look like an old FBI guy. It's our age, I think."

"No, no," Minihan said, "I'm talking about your outfit. All the Agency guys over there wear capes?"

"It's the continental look, Frank."

"You know what I think?" Minihan said. "I think that maybe compulsory euthanasia for the over-sixties has been inadequately explored as a solution to the Social Security deficit."

"Harsh stuff, Frank," Stuarti said. "You going to eat your doughnut?"

"Christ, no," Minihan said, "and it doesn't look like you need a second one, either."

Stuarti held the doughnut in both hands, like a raccoon, and regarded Minihan across it with bright eyes as he spoke.

"What's it been, Frank? Almost thirty years? You've got to expect that a man might put on a little weight."

"Thirty exactly," Minihan said, "I left Army Counterintelligence in fifty-six to come back and join the Bureau. You left Vienna and went back to Paris and stayed there, except maybe from sixty-one to sixty-three, when the record isn't real clear where you were."

"I still live there," Stuarti said. "Got a nice little place in the Latin Quarter." Stuarti brought the doughnut to his mouth with both hands and bit deeply. As he did so a blob of jelly popped softly out the far end of the doughnut and landed on his knee.

"Son of a *bitch*," Stuarti said.

"Number one, rue de Cardinale," Minihan said.

"This is a defective doughnut," Stuarti said, inspecting the end from which the jelly had exited. "You can kiss off that buck forty-five."

15

"And you've got an unlisted phone, which is 272-6458."

"What are you going to do, Frank, harass me on the overseas phone for a buck forty-five? I'd go back and talk to the guy that sold you the doughnuts, if I were you. Let me have your napkin."

"And while you've got a phone number," Minihan continued, "what you do not have is a GS number."

"Don't much miss it, either," Stuarti said.

"Thirty years a contract occasional, Ed? Jesus, either you've been doing a lot of things right or a lot of things wrong."

"Some of each," Stuarti said. "Do you know, I don't believe that I've been called Ed since I saw you last."

"That means no pension, right? Is that why you're still humping it around at your age instead of playing Bingo in the Home?"

"*Our* age," Stuarti said, "and no, I suppose if I wanted to go to the Merit Systems Protection Board, whine a little, they'd probably give me some money, if I needed it, or them, which I don't. Plus I've never been any good at the bureaucratic stuff, Frank. I'm an old agent runner, and I wouldn't like a desk."

"That's not quite the way I remember it, Ed," Minihan said after a pause. "I seem to remember that you were *very* good at the bureaucratic stuff."

"I'm a little better at it over there," Stuarti said mildly, "not so good at it over here."

There was a still longer pause before Minihan spoke again.

"What do they call you, if they don't call you Ed?"

"Monsieur Stuarti, mostly," Stuarti said, "Monsieur Edward if I've known 'em a long time."

"I've known you a long time. You want me to call you Mister Ed?"

"Nope. Ed's fine."

"Good. Now there were two things," Minihan said, "that definitely impressed me when the guy called me in two days ago, told me that I'd been asked for as Bureau liaison to an

16

interagency operation, said that you'd be in touch, and instructed me to offer all possible assistance.

"The first thing," he continued, "was that the guy was the assistant director. That impressed me right there. The second thing that impressed me was the fact that his instructions were verbal, no following memo, and the additional and worrisome fact that he didn't want to spend much time discussing the various possible definitions of all possible assistance."

"That's how you get to be assistant director," Stuarti said.

"And now," Minihan continued, "you start batting your eyes and making coy distinctions between over there and over here, and I get the same feeling I got when the A.D. took this one off *his* plate and put it on mine. I think that someone's going to ask me to break the law."

"Certainly not, Frank," Stuarti said, licking powdered sugar from his fingers.

"What *I* think," Minihan continued grimly, "is that your over here, over there distinction in matters bureaucratic is a not particularly veiled reference to the constitutional prohibition against Agency operations on domestic soil. Am I warm?"

"Let me tell you how I see the Constitution, Frank," Stuarti began brightly. "Now imagine that you've got a nine-to-five job, and you have to be there, every morning, right at nine."

"Easy," Minihan said, "I've got one just like that, had it for almost thirty years."

Stuarti shuddered visibly, then continued. "Imagine additionally, and of *course* hypothetically, that you roll in one night around three with a full tank and you've got to figure out how in hell you're going to get up at seven. Now if you keep the alarm clock right next to you, the minute it makes a peep you're just going to reach out, slap your hand on the snooze alarm, and keep it there 'til noon. *So*, being the crafty sort, what you do is put the alarm clock across the room, so

17

that you have to get up, shut it off. And it works. If you can walk, you must not be dead, might as well go to the office. By being both the manipulating and the manipulated party, you have successfully saved yourself from yourself. You with me?"

Minihan's face bleakened.

"What I'm saying, Frank, is that there's more than one way to look at the Constitution. Some people see it as a sacred document intended to protect ourselves from ourselves. *I* see it as an alarm clock set and put across the room by the Founding Fathers two hundred years ago. Now we both know that the only responsible government is contingent government, Frank, and that times change. A man has to set his own clock."

"I knew it," Minihan said glumly. "You *are* going to ask me to break the law. Might as well just go ahead and do it. What do you want?"

"More'n you can imagine, Frank," Stuarti said. "For starters, I'd like you to give me whatever the Bureau's got on the Fifteenth of June Group."

"Let me see if I've got it straight," Minihan said. "You, the Agency, would like us, the Bureau, to access the Octopus network of the National Crime Information Center and deliver to you classified information contained therein, contrary to statutory restrictions limiting such access to the Bureau, the Treasury Department, United States Army Counterintelligence, and the U.S. Customs Service. Is that it?"

"That's it," Stuarti said.

"Nope," Minihan said.

"What nope?" Stuarti said indignantly. "Didn't the guy tell you that that was one of the things I was going to ask for?"

"What he said, exactly," Minihan said, "was that you *might* ask about the Fifteenth of June Group, and that I *might* want to familiarize myself with the current file before we spoke. Now, unlike your adventuresome self, I *do* have a GS

18

number, a nice fat one in the teens, and the right to the pension that accrues thereto unless I step on my own toes in the next eighteen months, and when that slippery bastard says that I 'might' want to do this or that, it makes me nervous. What do you call that? Is that the conditional voice?"

"Got me," Stuarti said sulkily, "I'm a constitutional expert, not a grammarian. Besides, the prohibition isn't constitutional, anyway. It's just some nonsense in the charter."

"Will you stop *whining*," Minihan said. "I'm not saying I'm not going to help you. What I *am* saying is that I need to know a little more about the nature of your authority than the A.D. was willing to share with me."

"Actually, Frank," Stuarti said, "the authority is pretty nifty, and it was decided that we didn't need to trouble the A.D. with it."

"Trouble me with it."

"The charter giveth as well as taketh away, Frank," Stuarti said. "The clause we're concerned with here is a dandy little catchall at the end, which says that the Agency, in addition to its normal responsibilities—and I think I'm quoting this correctly here—'shall, in addition, discharge such other duties as the National Security Council may from time to time direct.'"

Minihan stared at Stuarti hard. "The National Security Council?"

"It's OK, Frank," Stuarti said cheerfully, "I wouldn't believe me, either. The director's expecting your call."

"I'm impressed, Ed," Minihan said, returning after a ten-minute absence. "I even told him you were dressed up like Rudolfo in some nursing home production of *La Bohème*, and all he did was groan and tell me to give you whatever you asked for."

"It's Blaine," Stuarti said. "That guy can really talk."

"The director *did* have a message," Minihan said, "only it struck me as a little oblique."

19

"What was it?"

"He said to 'tell those sandbagging cocksuckers that the goddamned rabbit is ours,' and to remind you that if anything happens to it that what he'll do to the Agency in front of a congressional oversight committee will make the Church hearings look like a valediction. He didn't sound all that happy."

"I'd heard that he was a little put out," Stuarti said.

"The National Security Council, eh?" Minihan mused aloud. "I'm a little scared to ask the next question, Ed."

"But you're going to anyway, I bet," Stuarti said.

"Yup," Minihan said. "What kind of godawful security problem can the nation have that, for its solution, requires the deputy director of operations not only to ring in the NSC, but to import for the occasion some antique art forger from the City of Light?"

"That's *dealer*, Frank," Stuarti said, "art *dealer*. Probably a translation mix-up."

"Tell Interpol," Minihan said. "It was their file I read, and my Larousse gives *faussaire* as forger. I've still got a question pending."

"The NSC authorization's just a rubber stamp, Frank," Stuarti said, waving a hand in vague dismissal. "Lets us work with the domestic agencies without having to worry about going to jail if something goes flooey . . ."

"Non-responsive, Ed."

". . . as for me, well, I've known Blaine a long time. Helped him cut his teeth when he was head of Paris station. We get along."

"Perhaps I should put the question another way, Ed," Minihan said after a pause.

"Sure," Stuarti said genially.

"What the hell was Dr. Walter Butterfield doing that made someone nervous enough to splatter his head all over the wall?"

"Butterfield?" Stuarti said, eyes wide. "The innocent by-stander?"

Minihan sighed. "I want you to remember two things, Ed, OK? First thing, it's against the law to lie to the FBI . . ."

"Always foremost in my mind, Frank."

". . . second thing, I'm on your side. I'm the guy that brought the jelly doughnuts, remember? Now the girl that made the call asked for Butterfield, not Porter. Mrs. Porter remembered that very clearly, and there's no reason in the world for her to make something like that up. That manifesto that the papers got was bullshit, but just because those silly bastards are all running around, sayin' stuff and pointing the way with the backs of their necks, doesn't mean we're *all* dummies. Now let me try again, and if you don't have it in you to give me a straight answer, maybe you could just clap faster if I'm getting warm. Butterfield worked for the Arms Control and Disarmament Agency. Do we have a problem at the ACDA?"

"Nothing *but* problems, Frank," Stuarti began earnestly. "In the past four years, measured in constant dollars, the ACDA's gross budget has been decreased by a third, the research portion slashed by more than eighty percent. What was, I understand, an impressive research library has been dispersed all over town, and their largest mainframe computer has been transferred to State, as rent, I suppose, for their pathetic office space."

"Ed . . ."

"Plus, in May '83 there was a reduction in authorized permanent staff from one ninety-nine to one fifty-four, the lowest level since 1962. In short, Frank, a troubled agency, with the budget of a large bookmobile, the technical support resources of a small mail-order operation, and, since Rostow was canned, the academic prestige of a Moroccan peg-house . . ."

"Stop it!" ordered Minihan.

21

"Yes," Stuarti said. "I'm afraid that we *do* have a small problem at the ACDA."

"Define small problem," said Minihan.

"It appears," Stuarti said, "that we may have a bad apple . . ."

"Define bad apple."

Here Stuarti paused, and when next he spoke his voice was flat and empty of banter.

" 'Soviet equity,' I believe, is the current bureaucratese," he said. "We used to call them 'assets.' Tell me about the Fifteenth of June Group."

"The Fifteenth of June Group," Minihan began, "consists of one guy and one girl, plus whoever they're screwing at the moment. They claim credit all over the place for stuff they didn't do, which is understandable, since their only verified exploits to date include two pipe bombs against apartheid, I think it was, one of which actually broke a window, and 'U.S. Out of Central America' spray-painted on the doors of Trinity Church."

"The guy is a Weinstein, Mark, deals grass out of his own apartment on West Nineteenth Street when he's not trying to get some broad to blow him because he's Che Guevara. Which of course he tells everyone he is. The girl is a Priscilla, No Last Name, cruises along behind Weinstein for the kinky sex. Which is what this is, sex games, not politics. On past form, there's no way in the world that those two featherheads could have done Butterfield the way that he was done."

"Actually, Frank," Stuarti said innocently, "that's pretty much the same conclusion that *we* came to . . ."

"Is that right?" Minihan asked.

"Sure," Stuarti said, showing some puzzlement at the absence of Minihan's irritation at being used as a confirmatory source. "Pick the Group's name out of the papers, use Porter's

22

house, throw in the 'manifesto' for a little extra smoke, and hope that Butterfield gets listed as an accident . . ."

"I'm afraid there's one problem with that analysis, Ed."

"Yes?" Stuarti said, suddenly alert. "What's that?"

"The girl that made the call to Butterfield."

"That's twice you've said girl," Stuarti said sharply. "How do we know it's a girl we're talking about, rather than a woman?"

"It *was* a girl," Minihan said. "Right now it's about a hundred and ten pounds of frozen meat on a gurney at St. Vinnie's."

"How can you know that she's the one that made the call?" Stuarti demanded.

"Made the call *and* planted the bomb," Minihan said. "Mrs. Porter picked her picture right out. And nothing against your analysis, Ed, but I'm afraid that she was also the one that Weinstein and his friend were screwing this month."

"The Fifteenth of June Group," Stuarti said accusingly. "You had 'em looped."

"If by looped," Minihan said, "you are suggesting that the Bureau availed itself of its legal right to nonconsensual electronic surveillance conducted under the Smith guidelines and pursuant to the warrant procedures and requirements of Title Three of the Omnibus Crime Control and Safe Streets Act of 1968, yeah, we had the shit looped out of them. But not a word anywhere about Butterfield, or Porter, or bad apples at the ACDA. At least not until yesterday."

"Yes?" Stuarti said.

Minihan bent to the briefcase at his feet and opened it. From it he withdrew a thick looseleaf binder with a green security cover sheet stamped COMINT and COMPARTMENTED.

"Transcripts from the tap on Weinstein's phone," Minihan said, turning to a flagged page near the end and handing the binder to Stuarti.

23

"Who's MV?" Stuarti asked.

"Male voice," Minihan said. "That's Weinstein. The female voice is our friend Priscilla."

The log summary information at the top of the page gave the day as Tuesday and the time as 10:20 A.M.:

FV: Hello?

MV: Yeah, it's me. Hey, listen . . .

FV: What time is it?

MV: Ten, eleven, I don't know. Listen, you see the papers this morning?

FV: Ten?

MV: Wake up, for Christ's sake! Fran's dead! It's in the *Post*! "Drugs Suspected in East Village Slaying." It's right in front of me! She's dead, is why she hasn't been answering the phone for three days! Drugs, my ass! That fucker Andreas killed her! We gotta . . .

FV: Where're you calling from?

MV: My place. I just got back with the paper. Listen to me . . .

FV: You're calling on your own phone?

MV: Yeah, big deal. Pay attention, for Christ's . . .

FV: You dumb shit.

CBD

"What's CBD?" Stuarti asked.

"Connection *broken* *distal*," Minihan said. "Means she hung up on him. The guy who designed the forms must have had two years of med school before he flunked out and joined the Bureau."

"Weinstein sounds a little nervous," Stuarti said, flipping through the following pages with an archivist's ease.

"Scared to death," Minihan agreed. "And not of the cops, either."

24

Stuarti abruptly stopped turning the pages and read for a moment in silence.

"Sounds like he decided to do something about it, too," he said softly.

The call that had caught Stuarti's attention had been made at 1:35 on the afternoon of the same day.

1MV: Hello?

2MV: Yeah, hello, is this Jack?

1MV: Who's calling?

2MV: Uh, am I talking to Jack?

1MV: Yeah. Who is this?

2MV: This is, uh, my name's Mark. Vinnie told me to call you. He said he talked to you yesterday, told you I was looking for something, and that you said maybe you could help me out.

1MV: *Who?*

2MV: Vinnie. From West Fourth Street. He said he talked to you yesterday.

1MV: Oh, OK, yeah, he did. Yeah, I can probably help you out, you gimme some idea a what you need.

2MV: Well, you know, pretty much anything you got. This, uh, I don't know too much about this, y'know? I just want something's gonna work, I need it to, and that I can carry without a holster.

1MV: Awright, listen. You know the Club Fifty-one, there, Sheridan Square?

2MV: Yeah.

1MV: You work in the afternoons, anything?

2MV: No.

1MV: Friday afternoon, then, say three o'clock. We can talk, and I can probably have something for you by then.

2MV: Listen, I, uh, that's three days from now, for Christ's sake!

1MV: That's right, my friend. It's, I figure, a guy who's in a big hurry for a piece is probably a guy who's already inna shit, and I don't need that. The stores got a good idea, the three days. Listen, look around. I'm gonna be there anyway, and if you don't show I'll figure you already picked something up. No skin off my ass either way.

2MV: Ah, shit. All right. Listen, uh, how am I gonna know you?

1MV: Well, it's not usually that crowded, three o'clock, y'know? You decide to show up, carry a *New York Times* and sit down near the phones. Nobody reads *The Times* in that shithole.

CBD

"The poor guy's hysterical," Stuarti said, "and everybody keeps hanging up on him. I wonder if Che Guevara had that problem."

"It's probably tough to take a guy seriously when he calls you up, tells you he wants a piece, and then says he'll take anything you've got," Minihan said. "I'm surprised the guy didn't tell him he'd give him ten percent off list on a six-inch Blackhawk, almost new, only been used to shoot four cops and a nun."

When Stuarti spoke again his tone was thoughtful.

"We agree, Frank, do we not, that this Weinstein and his girlfriend lack, at the very least, the technical resources to be plausible suspects in Butterfield's death?"

"Yes," Minihan said. "We do."

"Then perhaps," Stuarti said reflectively, "we should assume that maybe they've made a new friend recently. A *mean* new friend, with a knife and some ordnance expertise."

"Who's using the first name Andreas" Minihan said.

"Is that all we've got?" Stuarti asked. "The one mention of the name?"

"No," Minihan said.

26

"No?"

Minihan bent to his briefcase. When he straightened, he held a small cassette in his palm.

"We've got the girl who planted the bomb on tape," Minihan said. "The lab people got this off her answering machine. Her voice, plus a guy whose voice we hadn't heard before. The guys at Midtown South Homicide are calling him Mr. Badbar, but if Weinstein's right, we're listening to our friend Andreas."

"What do they talk about?" Stuarti asked.

"Installing and activating a bug," Minihan said. "It's kind of a short conversation."

"She didn't even know what she was doing," Stuarti said quietly. "Is that all?"

"No," Minihan said. "Then he guts her like a fish. She takes a little while to die. It's all on the tape."

Stuarti removed his glasses and rubbed his eyes with his thumb and forefinger, fatigue, or something like it, now evident in his face.

"Just out of curiosity, Frank," he asked, massaging the bridge of his nose, "does our friend Andreas have an accent?"

"German, we think," Minihan said.

"Anyplace special German?" Stuarti asked, his eyes still closed.

"Well, we've only got two sentences, so the analysts are guessing."

"What do they guess?"

"Thuringian or Saxon, seems to be the consensus," Minihan said. "Somewhere between Erfurt and Chemnitz, maybe."

"I think they call Chemnitz Karl-Marx-Stadt now, Frank," Stuarti said thoughtfully.

"I believe they do," Minihan said.

"I suppose," Stuarti said, "that if you ran around *long* enough telling everyone who'd listen that you were a bomb-throwing revolutionary, eventually someone besides the FBI might pay attention."

"Certainly a possibility," said Minihan.

"You might even make some new friends," Stuarti said.

"Why not?" Minihan agreed.

"And if one of your new friends turned out to be HVA," Stuarti said, referring to the Hauptverwaltung Aufklärung, the East German intelligence service, "sent as a favor to a large Eastern neighbor, well, you'd have to be real naive to be surprised."

"HVA," repeated Minihan softly. "I think maybe it's time for you to tell me a little more about our problem at the ACDA, Ed."

"I guess so," Stuarti said, painfully shifting position. "Perhaps we should transfer this discussion to a somewhat more secure venue, Frank. Somewhere where there's gin, say. Gimme your hand, help me out of this thing."

Minihan's eyes narrowed as Stuarti, pulling on Minihan's arm, rose to his feet and took several tentative steps, testing his legs for support.

"You can walk?" Minihan asked.

"Not far, not fast, and usually with a cane," Stuarti said, kicking a kink out of his right leg, "but I suppose you'd still call it walking."

"What is this?" demanded Minihan.

"It's a miracle, Frank," Stuarti said, folding his lap blanket over his arm. "The Blessed Virgin works in mysterious ways. Our Lady of the Incipient Pressure Sores. Get your coat."

"No, *this*," Minihan said, pointing accusingly to a tag attached to the rear of Stuarti's wheelchair.

The tag read TRANSWORLD AIRLINES COURTESY SERVICE.

"My legs always get stiff on planes," Stuarti said defensively.

"You *stole* this wheelchair?"

"For Christ's sake, Frank," Stuarti said. "We're concerned with national security here. This's no time to turn into an old lady. Where is your coat?"

CHAPTER FOUR

HIS control officer was already waiting on a stool at the counter of the Weinerwald on the corner of Eighth Street and University Place when the East German arrived at precisely 11:00 A.M. The control officer, heavyset and fiftyish, was wearing a suit of thick brown wool, light tan shoes, and yellow nylon socks that ended, visibly, two inches below the cuff. His hair, sprouting everywhere, was black, and that on his head glistened with a cream dressing. The East German, regarding him with distaste, had at their only previous meeting guessed him to be a Georgian.

Wearing a navy track suit and Adidas running shoes, the East German, who was as fair as the other man was dark, crossed to the counter and took the stool next to him. The older man hurriedly filled his mouth and crumpled a piece of wax paper as the East German seated himself.

"I am having a bun while I am waiting for you," the dark-haired man said, enveloping the East German in a cloud of carious breath and cologne. "Do you want lunch? I will pay."

"Coffee," the younger man said softly, looking down and grooming the blond hairs on his wrist.

"One coffee," the dark-haired man said to the waitress, "and I am having a Reuben sandwich.

"This is very good, a Reuben sandwich," he said confidingly to the younger man as the waitress departed. "A Jewish name, but still very good."

" 'I'll have . . .' or 'I'd like . . .' " the East German said stiffly; he had learned his American at the Fremdspracheninstitut at Jena, and was as proud of his grammar as he was painfully aware of his accent.

"What?" the dark-haired man demanded suspiciously.

"Nothing," the East German said, shaking his head and grimly recalling de Gaulle's definition of Europe as that area between the Atlantic and the Urals.

"Your friends are become famous," the dark-haired man said, now more softly, and then he winked grotesquely. "Maybe they hope they are going to Hollywood!"

The East German said nothing.

"So your little girl did very well, then," the dark-haired man said, his smile fading in the face of the East German's silence.

"Yes," the East German said. "The unit was modular, and required only that she unplug the current handset and substitute the new one. We practiced many times." In the context, he was uncertain of his use of 'current,' and immediately regretted having used the word.

The waitress brought the coffee and sandwich, of which the dark-haired man ate half before he spoke again.

"And she is dead now?" the dark-haired man said to his plate, now very softly indeed.

"Yes," the East German said, raising his eyes and for the first time turning his gaze on his interlocutor. "She is."

"There are only the other two, then, who have met you?" the dark-haired man said, ending his sentence on an interrogative note in default of the proper construction.

"Yes," the East German said.

"It is decided that they, also, should be dead," the man

30

said, removing a toothpick crowned with green paper from the second sandwich half. "This we expected, yes?"

"Yes," the East German said.

"Do you need any . . ."

"No," the East German said.

"When?" the dark-haired man demanded flatly. "I am asked to report everything."

"Now," the East German said, his voice unchanging.

"Now?" the older man repeated stupidly. He was genuinely startled, and his hand involuntarily covered the uneaten portion of his sandwich.

Noticing the dark-haired man's gesture, the East German mistook the tone for mockery and was instantly furious. Did the fat fool not know that "now" could refer as correctly to the immediate future as to the present moment? For an instant he was conscious in his arm and shoulder of a desire to strike the man, to knuckle-punch him in the temple, to drive the thin bone into the brain and the fat body from its stool.

"Now," he repeated icily. "I am going there now."

Leaving a dollar on the counter by his cup, the East German turned and left. His stride was light as he crossed the street, and his fair hair shone in the morning sun.

It was a twenty-minute walk from Eighth Street and University Place to the East Village tenement building that was the East German's destination. From the bustle of bookstores, record shops, and storefront Tofutti stands, he passed into a landscape increasingly lunar. The disease he sensed everywhere latent in the city was here more advanced, its chancres more naked. Dead, blind buildings began to appear among those still barely living, here and there the corpses of cars. The street population became increasingly Hispanic. On the corners, watching, young Negro men stood silently in groups of three or four.

As he walked, the East German was aware in himself of an utter inability to imagine the histories or habits of this

31

lumpen population, to narrate to himself a possible individual life. This sense of narrative impotence made him uneasy, and he began to fear, and thus to despise, the dark-skinned rabble about him. The process of hardening himself through fear and hate was a familiar one, and he deliberately allowed the emotion to grow as he walked, opening unchecked within him like a poisonous nightflower.

By the time he reached his destination on Sixth Street east of Avenue A, therefore, and entered the dimly lit hallway cluttered with empty cardboard boxes, he had come wholly to focus. Once inside, he would quarrel with the man and strike him. He would then turn to the girl, calm her with a smile, and kill her before returning to the man on the floor. This he would do to protect himself, and without compunction, for though the man and woman were white of skin, they were Negroes as surely as those east of lower Fifth Avenue, or as those east of the Urals.

The third-floor door was sheathed in sheet metal. The girl who opened it was blond and petite, wore overalls and a white T-shirt above bare feet, and held the stub of a joint burned almost to her fingers.

"*An*-dy!" she said in a teasing singsong voice as she closed the door behind him, the bar of the police lock rattling. "Does anybody call you Andy, Andy?"

The East German's eyes swept the room. There was no one else there. He was conscious of a moment of collapse, within.

"No," he said. "Where is Mark? He was to be here."

The girl crossed the room, taking three short puffs on the roach before dropping it into a brimming ashtray, grimacing, and shaking her fingers. For a moment she held the smoke, and then exhaled it, slowly.

"I don't think Markie's coming today," she said, smiling at the East German. "I talked to him on the phone and everything, and I think maybe he's afraid of you."

"Afraid?" the East German repeated carefully.

32

"Yeah," the girl said, holding him with her eyes. "He thinks you killed Fran, and it's like, it's making him a little nervous."

The East German, who had not seen the article in the newspapers although he thought he had read them closely, was badly startled and struggled for a moment.

"Why?" he demanded. "Why does he think that?"

"Did you?" the girl asked, still smiling.

The East German, composed again, looked straight at the girl and nodded, once. "She did not know what she was doing," he said. "She might have contacted the police when she found out that it was not a listening device. She had no strength. She could not be trusted."

"I dunno," the girl said, her smile eerily undimmed. "She would of had to look up the number, and I'm not sure Fran could do that. I suppose she coulda called 911, though. Did you fuck her?"

"No," the East German said, clearly receiving an A for his answer. "She was not serious."

"And how about me?" the blond girl said, unclipping her overalls and letting them fall. "Am I serious?"

Touching her, he found her already excited, an excitement, he would have been startled to know, that derived not from the sexual frissons of betrayal and murder, nor from the conspiratorial appeal of mazes and techniques, but rather from her sudden conviction, born only moments before, that he was homosexual.

The East German's thoughts, as he stroked her, were more simple. He could not kill them both today. He would therefore have to kill them both another day. As soon as possible.

ASAP.

In America, a country hurtling to its historical consummation, the letters alone sufficed.

CHAPTER FIVE

THE "more secure venue" to which Stuarti and Minihan retired from the field office on Centre Street was on Hudson Street south of Horatio, and was named Bar. No tables were occupied save the one at which Stuarti and Minihan sat, and their only companions were the bartender and two unshaven old men at the rail, all drinking eight-ounce glasses of draft beer and watching "The Dating Game." The room smelled foully of urinal cakes and stale ashtrays.

"Nice place, Frank," Stuarti said mildly, sipping, now, his second drink. "Lot of gin."

"It smells like a men's room in here," Minihan said, warily regarding the scum on his instant coffee.

"I know," Stuarti said contentedly, *"homey."*

"There's going to have to be a contact report for the files, Ed," Minihan said, shuddering, "and if it's going to justify the level of resources I have the feeling you're going to ask for, it'll have to show a bit more supporting detail than I've got so far. Like to tell me a little bit about Butterfield's discovery?"

On the television above Minihan's head, a peroxide blond identified as "a skin-diver, gourmet cook, and ex-cheer-leader" was posing questions to three men hidden behind a screen. "If I were a lawn," she asked sweetly, "would you roll me, water me, or fertilize me? Number One?" "Well, Susan," the first of the three hidden men responded in a tone of measured deliberation, as though the question were not insane, "I suppose that I'd just have to rely on *you* to tell me which you needed most."

A thoughtful pout from Susan. Mild audience applause.

Returning his attention from the television to Minihan, Stuarti sat back and tented his chubby fingers in rich anticipation, for though he had read the file's technical appendices only once, two weeks before, he had a lovely memory which, in the presence of his contemporaries, was a source of private vanity.

"Three hints," Stuarti began. "First hint—though we didn't recognize it as such at the time—was picked up by NSA nine months ago," he said. "Report dated twelve July last year, unbuttoning of a SIGINT intercept taken on nine July by a new rhomboid array set up to monitor communications between the Soviet embassy and the East Sixty-seventh Street mission in New York. It was a squirt, so they didn't get it all, but the analysts are pretty sure it involved instructions for the forthcoming meeting of the Standing Consultative Commission on compliance with the SALT II Accords. Nothing fancy, just a proposed agenda, but an agenda that, oddly, indicated inclusion of Soviet objections to encryption of telemetry data on tests of the Pershing-2s . . ."

". . . a *lawn?*" said Number Two.

"What's odd about that?" Minihan asked.

"We aren't doing it," Stuarti said. "Haven't done it in the past, aren't doing it now, don't have any plans to start. And, sure enough, they brought it up anyway."

"Sounds like they got some bad information," Minihan said, shrugging.

"Second hint," Stuarti continued, beginning to hit stride, "came two months ago in an article in the journal of the

Soviet general staff, *Voennaya Mysl'*. The article was concerned with current levels of U.S. STEALTH aircraft technology, and assumed a current capacity, *production* capacity, of anechoic technology adequate to reduce a radar signature by a factor in excess of twenty . . ."

". . . plough you from end to end and fertilize your *socks* off, Susan baby . . ."

"Where the hell did you learn this gobbledygook?" Minihan demanded indignantly. "You *used* to talk like a normal person . . ."

"It gets worse."

". . . now it's 'rhomboid arrays,' 'encryption of telemetry data,' 'Vienna missiles', 'radar signatures' . . ."

"*Voennaya Mysl'* . . ."

"Whatever. Listen, Ed, you said it yourself, I'm an old FBI guy. You want to talk about Ma Barker, maybe, or the Lindbergh baby, I'm your man. Vienna missiles, forget it . . ."

"Will you just cut the old fart act and *listen*," Stuarti said impatiently. "Like the assumption of planned telemetry encryption, this information is *also* wrong. I'm told that our current levels of anechoic technology, even testing levels, can reduce a signature by a factor of maybe eight, ten tops. That's being *extremely* wrong."

"I don't want to seem overly critical, Ed," Minihan said sullenly, "but as enlightening hints go, your first two suck. That's a lay opinion, of course."

Behind Minihan the television erupted in wild applause and harsh cries of envy as "The Dating Game" 's host advised Susan and Number Three, the rapist chosen for her by the show's producers, to "pack your swimsuits for a long weekend in fabulous . . . *San Juan, Puerto Rico!*" Susan, good sport to the end, was doing her best to hop up and down with joy, but her squeals betrayed a discernible edge of fear, and the proprietary necklock in which the rapist now casually held her made hopping difficult.

"Then cheer up, Frank," Stuarti said, "The third one should clear everything up."

"Good," Minihan said.

"Do you know much about mathematical modeling?" Stuarti asked.

"No," Minihan said, glaring, "of course not."

"Correlation models?" Stuarti demanded. "Game theory? Harsanyi's Postulate? The Zeuthen-Nash Theory of Bargaining? Nonsymmetrical move structures in mixed-motive games?"

"No," Minihan gritted.

"Me neither," Stuarti continued brightly, "but Butterfield did. Turns out he headed the Modeling and Gaming Group within ACDA. Now when the Agency went through its post-Rostow reorganization—and lost its only mainframe to State, you'll recall—the Modeling and Gaming Group, in order to get adequate machine time, got bounced up here to New York to the Courant Institute of Mathematics at NYU. An elite group, Frank. Six loonies and a giant computer, and what they do, as best I understand it, is answer hypothetical questions. Like, 'If we pattern-bomb Yakutsk with Chicken McNuggets, will we win the hearts and minds of the people?' And Butterfield's boys ask the computer: tappety-tap, tappety-tap, nope, Siberians don't like chicken. OK, the planners ask, what about Reese's Pieces instead of McNuggets? Tappety-tap, and the model spits out f-levels of significance for Reese's Pieces. Playing with the variables, Frank. Doesn't mean we're going to do it, we might not even have a delivery system capable of getting the McNuggets there hot, but the model still lets us explore the possibilities. You OK, Frank?"

"God's mercy on a tired old man," moaned Minihan. "F-levels of significance for Reese's Pieces?"

"Attaboy," Stuarti said, "Now . . ."

"Where the hell did you ever hear of Chicken McNuggets?" demanded Minihan.

"I may be an expatriate," Stuarti said in a tone of offended dignity, "but I'm also an American, and I keep up with the important stuff. Fast foods, used car prices, the activities of the Kennedys . . . the *Herald Tribune*'s got it all. Now, Butterfield is a diligent fellow, does his homework, and reads all the relevant professional journals. Three weeks ago he got to the issue of *Voennaya Mysl'* that I mentioned, the one with the article inexplicably assuming an anechoic technology capacity adequate to reduce a radar signature by a factor of twenty. An hour later he was in Mac Reynold's office—you know him, right, the Chief of Security at INR?—"

"Yes," Minihan said.

". . . with a possible, and worrisome, explanation. It seems that five months ago Butterfield's boys were working on a STEALTH model that assumed, hypothetically, a signature reduction capacity of precisely twenty-two."

"Coincidence, maybe?" Minihan asked, the sound of the TV suddenly more distant.

"Could be," Stuarti said. "Thing is, ten months ago his little group was playing with a bargaining model on SALT compliance that assumed encryption of all telemetry data on tests of the Pershing-twos. Another drink?"

His glass refreshed, his admiration for the bartender's skillful professionalism in mixing ice and gin lavishly expressed, and a second coffee for Minihan declined, Stuarti began, for Minihan's benefit, to rehearse the arithmetic.

"When we first began counting on our fingers," he said, "the numbers seemed daunting. Product-cleared customers on the two distribution lists numbered forty-two. With secretaries, P.A.'s, and whatnot, that number got puffed up to fifty-eight. Add Butterfield's six analysts, plus clerical and programming staff in Washington of thirty-one and in New York of thirteen, and we were looking at more than a hundred possibles. At first glance, that would seem a very comfortable crowd in which to get lost."

"Yes?" Minihan said, sensing that Stuarti's presentation was a set piece that would more rapidly proceed to its conclusion without interruption.

"In fact," Stuarti continued, "the security of the crowd proved to be illusory. First, the distribution lists for the two products were entirely different, which allowed us to exclude the customers, and thereby assume the problem to be internal to Butterfield's group. That still would have left us with fifty or so. Happily, and quite unforseeably, the clerical and support staff who worked on the SALT model didn't make the move to New York—no money in the new budget for relocation allowances—"

"Which, if I'm not missing something," Minihan said sharply, "leaves us with Butterfield's original six analysts . . ."

"Actually," Stuarti murmured, "we were able to cut it a bit finer than that."

"How fine?" asked Minihan quietly.

"We allowed ourselves to assume that our . . . candidate . . . was unaware of the reorganization plans within the Agency until they were made public," Stuarti said. "Otherwise he would have known that the partial move to New York would have left him a bit naked and made some provision in that regard."

"How many of the six . . ."

"Two," Stuarti said. "Butterfield's senior systems analyst and the guy who conducted the negotiations with the Courant Institute."

"Leaving four," Minihan said, almost to himself.

"You'll recall, Frank," Stuarti continued, "that the information in the two leaks we picked up was not only wrong, but militarily improbable. Impressive to the cleaning lady, maybe, or to some poor, unsophisticated systems analyst, but quite obvious as mere test variables, I'm told, to anyone with prior Defense Department experience."

"Go ahead," Minihan said.

"Of the remaining four candidates," Stuarti said, "one is on loan from the Air Force, and two of the others came from the Pentagon's Studies and Gaming Agency . . ."

"Oops," breathed Minihan.

". . . leaving us with Butterfield's deputy head of Section for Administration. A data base specialist, whatever *that* might be, and newly employed, hired as a consultant thirteen months ago . . ."

Here Minihan suddenly interrupted, frowning and shaking his head.

"Too many assumptions, Ed," he objected, "too loosely based."

"Yes," Stuarti agreed equably, "I suppose so."

"You've found a place to start, maybe," Minihan said reprovingly, "but as far as presentable evidence goes you've got nothing, not even the most circumstantial . . ."

"Oh," Stuarti said lightly, in that tone of mild innocence often affected by debaters who know themselves to be holding trumps, "I'd say we've got a dozen or so pieces of very compelling circumstantial evidence indeed."

"Where?" demanded Minihan.

"In a baggie, at the moment," Stuarti said.

"I beg your pardon?"

"Butterfield's head."

"I'm waiting," snapped Minihan.

"Last Tuesday," Stuarti said evenly, "at our instruction, and making it clear that he had not previously broached the topic elsewhere, Butterfield confided his concern about the *Voennaya Mysl'* article to his new deputy head of Section. A cautious fellow, his deputy, who warned Butterfield, for the sake of an already troubled agency, against precipitate action, and suggested that they meet the following Saturday, on his return from Washington, and go over the data again together before bothering the security people. Butterfield, unfortunately, didn't make the meeting. Got his head blown off the night before."

40

The traffic noises outside seemed suddenly muted, more distant, as the two old men regarded one another in silence.

"Could I have a yes or no answer to my next question, Ed?"

"Sure," Stuarti said.

"Are you telling me officially that the Soviets currently have an agent in place at a senior level of the Arms Control and Disarmament Agency, *and that you know who it is?*"

"Nope," Stuarti said, "officially we aren't even having this conversation."

"And unofficially?"

". . . Tessie Horowitz, *come on down!*" screamed a voice on the television.

"We call him Bunny," Stuarti said shyly, his tone one of almost paternal pride.

Over the next thirty minutes Stuarti outlined to Minihan the nature of the Bureau support that the contact report would show to have been requested.

For the record, it was agreed that the Bureau would maintain full physical and electronic surveillance of code-name Bunny with the stated objective of discerning the method of product delivery and identifying the servicing courier or couriers—"cutouts," in the jargon. Stuarti's insistence on a minimum of four new faces per four-hour shift with a two-car backup at all times and a rollover of no less than three days meant that the physical surveillance alone would require a dedicated personnel force in excess of seventy, a contingent adequate not only to maintain surveillance without risking a familiar face, but also, as the director later remarked sourly to Minihan, to guarantee the Bureau's formal—indeed, primary —role in the investigation should a congressional oversight committee be inclined to inquire.

For the record, it was further agreed, the initiation of electronic surveillance, both the tapping of the telephones used by code-name Bunny and the spiking of his home and office, would await the establishment of the statutorily mandated Pen Registers, summary logs, and renewable warrants, though in this regard Stuarti observed that he would not be displeased were such surveillance to start "yesterday;" an odd remark, Minihan thought briefly, for someone familiar with the rules of evidence to make were successful prosecution the ultimate intention.

Off the record, Stuarti had three favors to ask.

"What are they?" Minihan demanded.

"First," Stuarti said, "I'd like you to give this Weinstein and his girlfriend a good leaving alone for the next few days. Keep the wires on, but otherwise give them room. And keep their new friend off the record, even as speculation, for the time being. I've got a ferret of my own to put down that particular hole, and I wouldn't want him biting some FBI guy by mistake."

"No problem," Minihan said.

"Second," Stuarti said, "I need a back-dated CS number for a guy. You still designate your informants with confidential source numbers?"

"Yup," said Minihan. "Who's the guy?"

"My ferret," Stuarti said. "He goes about six-one, one-ninety, and the hole is small and shitty. It's possible he might get some on him, and if he does it'd be nice if he could cross his heart, say he was working for his uncle, and have the Bureau records back him up."

"Nicer than having to say he works for the Agency and getting Congress all upset, I suppose," Minihan said.

"That's it," Stuarti said cheerfully.

"What's the third one?" Minihan asked.

"That gun dealer that Weinstein was talking to," Stuarti said, "the one named Jack. Think you could get a last name and an address for him in the next twenty-four hours?"

"There're a lot of guys selling guns," Minihan shrugged, "but if he hangs out regularly in the Club Fifty-one I imagine

42

we could make him pretty fast. I'll talk to a couple of detectives I know in the Sixth."

"Let's try hard," Stuarti said. "I'd like the guy picked up sometime early Friday morning, nice and quietly, no fuss, no noise."

"Yes?" Minihan said.

"Why not?" said Stuarti. "As long as Weinstein's willing to go out on blind dates, I think maybe I'll see if I can't fix him up with my ferret."

Leaving the bar, Stuarti walked slowly with Minihan two blocks to Abingdon Square, where, on the corner of Twelfth Street and Eighth Avenue, Minihan caught an uptown cab. Declining the offer of a lift, Stuarti waited, waving, until Minihan's cab was out of sight, then carefully crossed the avenue and entered the Jackson Square Pharmacy.

To his enormous irritation, the pharmacy did not stock walking canes of any sort, much less the black thorn he favored, obliging him finally, and gracelessly, to settle for a pair of aluminum forearm crutches.

Inexpert in their use, Stuarti emerged from the pharmacy with an odd, scuttling gait, the thin metal supports rapidly stabbing the pavement as his large head swiveled about in search of a cab.

Ambulatory, and with his beret now in the pocket of his cape, Stuarti no longer looked like the tragically paralyzed Rudolfo his appearance had suggested to Minihan.

Now he looked like an arachnoid Oscar Wilde.

No one in Abingdon Square paid him the least attention.

CHAPTER SIX

IN a small cottage in Connecticut's northwest corner two hours from New York, Tom Matthews, who did not look like a ferret at all—indeed, with his short graying hair and wire glasses, rather more like an incongruously muscled Latin teacher at a boy's preparatory school—quietly hung up the phone having agreed to hunt a man to the death.

This was something that he very much did not wish to do; the prospect filled him with a bleakness close to dread. Further, the request fell well outside the purview of his current contractual obligations as an I-6 security officer of the Central Intelligence Agency; duty as defined by job description had no part in his decision at all, and when Stuarti closed a conversation by saying "Please be careful, dear boy," the words had a very different reasonance than a similar admonition from one's mom. What, then, might one speculate about his motive in agreeing without demur to do so?

In his classic analysis of the Battle of Agincourt, the military historian John Keegan attempts to isolate those factors which, taken separately or severally, provide what he calls the Will to Combat. Of the constituent elements that he identifies, five predominate: strong drink, the endorsement of religion within the circumscription of the just war, the possibility of personal enrichment through the taking of hostages, the commonplace character of violence in medieval life, and the personal bond between leader and follower.

Strong drink played no role in Matthew's decision. No more did religious conviction, for though his commitment to the values and forms of Western liberalism was strong and unashamedly normative, he was, at forty, far too old for crusades and had long ago ceased believing that his norms were anything more than, simply, his. The possibility of personal enrichment was likewise irrelevant. His salary sufficed for his unclamorous material needs—indeed, had bought the cottage in which he now stood—and Matthews no longer took prisoners. And while the will and recourse to violence as a disturbingly constant option in Matthew's life might have borne, just at that moment, more scrutiny than the other factors, it could not properly be granted the status of a motive force.

Elimination, therefore, suggests that it is to that personal bond between leader and follower, which Keegan asserts lies at the root of all explanations of what does and does not happen in battle, that one might best look for an answer, and looking, find it.

For it was Stuarti who had recruited Matthews in Paris more than fifteen years before.

Matthews had been a graduate student in political science attending the lectures of Raymond Aron. One evening, returning to his small apartment in the Marais, Matthews had been insulted by a drunken Tunisian outside the Métro St. Paul. Misled by Matthews's seeming passivity in the face of his *enguelade*, the Tunisian had pulled a knife, to further intimidate and humiliate.

Matthews had broken both his arms.

Already aware of Matthews's name, and intrigued by the fact of the second arm, Stuarti had accompanied the consular official to the Commissariat du Temple where Matthews was being held, intervened with the *juge d'instruction* on his behalf, and invited him to his home for dinner.

Stuarti's apartment in the rue de Cardinale had in the years since the war become legendary in the European intelligence community. Nominally (and budgetarily) a safe house, it had served for three decades as a salon for spies, its address more widely known to foreign intelligence services than that of the Georges V.

It is an intelligence cliché that a good agent must have entertainment value and Stuarti, as a homosexual expatriate, master gossip, and dealer in questionable art, most surely had that. Carried (at his own insistence) as a contract occasional, Stuarti had run his odd salon like a well-managed casino; brokering deals, exchanging gossip, providing a venue for informal discussions, and, by virtue of his institutional advantage as host, always and unobtrusively taking down a small informational percentage for the house. The occasional bit of talent-spotting, too, fell within his self-defined brief, and within the month—recognizing a natural when he saw one—Stuarti had obtained the necessary POA (Provisional Operational Approval) from CS counterintelligence and had pitched Matthews, cold.

It was Stuarti, too, following Matthews's stateside Junior Officer Training, who had arranged his transfer from Analysis and Estimate, to which his languages and academic credentials had caused him to be assigned, to KUDESK (EE) (Bloc Operations Division of Clandestine Services), the bureaucratic entity to which Stuarti nominally reported.

In the decade that followed, what had begun as a professional relationship gradually deepened into friendship. Matthews, always an alert student, adopted Stuarti as his teacher and mentor, treating the older man with a nearly filial deference and affection. Stuarti, for his part, occasionally glimpsed in Matthews an earlier, unchosen self, in which an unstained sense of obligation, of unpaid debt, provided the motive to service. Stuarti treasured this in Matthews, and if he had accepted at face value Matthews's explanation of his sudden transfer sixteen months prior to I-6 security—"time for a rest and retread"—rather than identify it as a last and desperate response to that final fatigue for which in field work there is no cure, he may be forgiven, for the love of an adoptive father can blur for a moment even the clearest vision.

Loyalty as a norm, therefore, held for them both a status that others might accord to honor or to love, and if in his brief conversation with Stuarti Matthews had been less than wholly forthcoming about his current circumstances, it was only out of another, more recent, loyalty; one irrelevant, as he chose to see it, to Stuarti's needs.

Her name was Kate.

Her eyes were blue, her hair was black, and she was that afternoon at a local hospital, having the casts removed from her hands.

CHAPTER SEVEN

ON the day that the casts were removed from Kate's hands, spring arrived like a carnival hitting town unannounced.

Save the Kodachrome robins on the kitchen calendar, there had been little hint of its advent. Even that morning had dawned gray and chill, a raw wind scudding the stacked clouds above the leafless hills, and thus it seemed to Kate a small miracle to emerge from the Sharon Medical Arts Building—from the whine and dust of the surgical saw, the stink of stale bandages, and the shock of scars she had only before imagined—into a day of melting air and brilliant blue, rich with the expectancy of a new season, with cloud tatters racing against a sky of lapis lazuli and the light, suddenly everywhere, proclaiming itself, with the psalmist, to be the outer garment of God.

Kate sat quietly in her car for a few minutes, breathing deeply and regarding her hands, then briskly brushed her hair and perfumed her neck and wrists, for she had promised the retarded children at the school where she now taught, who knew she was going to the doctor that day and thus were apprehensive on her behalf, that she would stop by that afternoon as proof that the doctor had not decided, as doctors were commonly known to do, that a change of institution would be beneficial.

Driving to the school over the country roads of Connecticut's northwest hills (still steering, from habit, with her thumbs), Kate lowered the driver's window and the car filled instantly with spring noise, the ditches alive with overflow and gurgle, the newly arrived birds yammering like conventioneers. The children had been shepherded onto the lawn for sun, and on her arrival flocked to her, their pear-shaped bottoms and waddling Mongoloid gait giving them the air of amiable baby ducks, all calling frantically, "Miss Farrington! Miss Farrington!" which was the name by which the school knew her.

With lively curiosity and grave solicitude, the children examined her new hands, touching and kissing the livid surgical zippers and clucking at the single finger that would neither close nor straighten. One child wept, mourning, as it turned out, the athletic socks that she had that winter worn as mittens.

In answer to their questions Kate patiently explained, for what might have been the thousandth time, that the scars, like the casts, were the result of a car accident in which her hands had been pinched. This she did unblushingly, though both "accident" and "pinch" were retrospective aggrandizements, her hands having been quite deliberately slammed in a car door, twice each.

The cottage where Kate had spent the last four months was on a hill overlooking the Housatonic River Valley, down which in winter the northern air had rolled without cease, flattening the burdock and thistle that in summer would rise to the sills, and bringing snowstorms from the Berkshires that from her porch she could watch forming in Massachusetts an hour before they arrived.

During her morning's absence, Kate noticed (with wonder, for she was a city girl) that the yard had started spring without

49

her. The earth, still that morning sodden and bleak beneath the heavy sky, now suddenly exhaled a vital fragrance of leaf decay and damp as potent as woodsmoke. The wild forsythia, at breakfast a tangle of dead sticks bordering the lane, was now visibly hazed with green, and crocuses, an unanticipated delight, rose everywhere, even beneath the spruce boughs where the last remnants of the defeated snow lay, vivid blue in shadow.

As she entered the cottage, Kate could hear from the back yard the sound of a maul striking wood, and crossing to the kitchen window she gazed into the back yard where Tom Matthews, her love and her mystery—though the record showed him only as her case officer—was splitting chunks of red oak for her stove.

Matthews was tall, fair, and forty. His hair was short, more gray than blond, and he wore a sweatband ripped from an old towel to keep his glasses clear. In a suit, Kate knew, he was capable of looking slender, but beneath the sweat-soaked T-shirt that he now wore the thick muscles of his back stood out in slabs.

In the first two months that she had been there Matthews had come every weekend, arriving each Saturday morning in a rented car with New York plates and leaving in the evening after supper. He left no personal possessions of his own, not even a book or a toothbrush, and once, when she had spoken of her second coffee mug as his, he had the same morning bought her a set of six, which he thereafter used varyingly.

Then in January he had disappeared, neither coming nor calling, and Kate, bereft, would have thought herself abandoned had she not learned from Mrs. Mulready, retained at Matthews's insistence to help her with the cleaning and washing up, that he spoke to Mr. Mulready daily, though on what subject his wife, who had been sworn to secrecy, could not say.

He had returned on a February Saturday, without apology

and with an odd reluctance. Pale, gaunt, distracted, he explained that he had had a fibroid cyst excised and had been ill. Kate had wept with happiness at his return—the first time he had seen her cry—and that night they had become lovers. That night, too, Kate had found the fresh scars (for there were two) of Matthews's recent surgery: a small neat round one low on the left side of his abdomen and a larger, more irregular wound low on the left back. Kate did not remark on this anomaly, though she too had once had a cyst removed and the process had not entailed an exit wound.

Matthews had spent that night and the next. On the third day, feverish and with a thin discharge seeping from the wound in his back, he had attempted to leave and they had argued, Kate with a dogged and unshakable tenacity that had dissolved into tears only when he was at last asleep in her bed. The six weeks that had followed, Matthews mending daily in her care, had been the happiest time of Kate's life.

"Tom!" she called from the open window, her hands hidden by the sill, "I'm home!"

Driving the maul into the splitting stump, Matthews turned, smiled, and started toward the house.

"Wait!" she cried, her heart suddenly in her throat. "Wait until I call you! I have a surprise."

Turning from the window and pulling her sweater over her head (realizing joyfully as she did so that blouses with buttons were no longer an impossibility), Kate raced upstairs and ran herself a tub full of water as hot as she could bear.

Blue-eyed, pink-nippled, her fine black pubic bush floating proudly like a silken nimbus at the tip of her slender body, Caitlin O'Kearney, naked in her bath, was more convincingly Irish than her name. After a long soak, she topped the tub again with hot, and washed herself with a lingering and luxurious intimacy that had not been possible in the months that

51

her hands had been chunks of concrete wrapped in Glad bags against the damp.

Only then did she call Matthews.

"Look, Ma," she said with determined gaiety, stepping naked from the tub, "new hands!" and when Matthews wordlessly held out his broad flat palms she placed her hands in his, scars up, without hesitation or self-consciousness. He held them gently for a long moment without speaking, and when finally he said, "I'm sorry," his hurt was so evident that she would have taken her hands back, hidden them forever, had it not meant releasing his.

Drying Kate, as was often the case, took longer with two than with one, obliging her finally, when she feared her legs might no longer hold her, to solemnly observe that "the more you dry it, the wetter it gets," which paradox they adjourned to the bedroom to celebrate.

It was dusk when Kate woke to find Matthews sitting on the edge of the bed, fully dressed, his hand on her cheek stroking her awake.

"Where are you going?" she demanded, her heart suddenly too large for her chest. "What are you doing?"

"I have to go," Matthews said softly, answering neither question.

"They called again, didn't they?" Kate demanded.

"They?" teased Matthews gently.

"Your CIA colleague from Paris," Kate said. "The one who called the other day."

"More old friend than CIA colleague," Matthews said, "and yes, he did. He's in New York."

"And you told him that you were leaving that business," Kate said, her voice as level as she could make it. "That you were looking for another job."

"No," Matthews said. "I didn't tell him that."

"Why not?" cried Kate. "It's true!"

"As you said," Matthews said, standing, "he's an old friend," and there was in his tone a quiet earnestness that precluded further argument.

"Then hurry back," Kate said finally, determined not to weep.

"And be careful," she said, as she stood by the car.

Because I love you more than life, she said, but by then the car had disappeared into the lowering dusk, and he was gone.

Chapter Eight

THE safe house that would serve as the command post for Stuarti and the interagency group was a single-family brownstone on Thirteenth Street west of Sixth Avenue.

It was shortly before nine in the morning when an unsmiling crew-cut young man wearing a three-piece brown suit and a military .45 in a shoulder holster showed Matthews into the living room.

Stuarti, robed in a high-collared mandarin dressing gown buttoned to the chin, sat hunched in the TWA wheelchair, his lap filled with papers, and books stacked high to either side of the chair.

"Dear *boy*," Stuarti said, his face brightening as Matthews entered. "*Long* time, no see."

"Do you want me to stay?" the young man asked, not taking his eyes from Matthews.

"*No*," Stuarti said sternly.

"I'll be right outside, then," the young man said grimly.

"Why don't you just pop down to Balducci's," Stuarti suggested as the young man turned to leave, "and get us some more of that fresh orange juice."

"I can't do that, Mr. Stuarti, sir," the young man said.

"Floyd's a Mormon," sighed Stuarti by way of explanation, well before the door had closed behind the young man. "For some reason Blaine thought I needed one, and wouldn't take no for an answer."

In addition to Stuarti and his books, the room contained only two camp beds, a TV, a bank of four color-coded telephones on one card table and a computer terminal and acoustic coupler on another. Seating himself on one of the beds, Matthews shrugged off his windbreaker and put the small gym bag he had brought with him on the floor by his feet.

"That wheelchair yours, Mary?" he asked, using Stuarti's work name, from habit.

"Certainly not," Stuarti said indignantly. "Handy little items, though. I've even been thinking about getting one of my own."

"Still the arthritis?" Matthews asked.

"That," Stuarti said, "and about ninety-five other things. Yeats must have already been senile when he wrote 'Sailing to Byzantium.' If *my* soul tried to clap its hands every time it found a new tatter in its mortal dress, its goddamned palms'd be bleeding. And you, dear boy?"

"Oh, you know," Matthews smiled. "Not bad. How's Arthur?"

"Not good," Stuarti said, shaking his head sadly. "He wore his Madame de Staël outfit to David Hall's bal masqué in the Marais, and insisted on wearing heels even though the goddamned dress comes to the floor. Caught a heel in his hem on David's first-floor landing and rolled all the way into the Place des Vosges. Broke his hip. They say he'll be able to manage a walker, but when I went out to Neuilly to see him he looked like he was headed for that great Coppet in the sky."

"I'm sorry to hear that," Matthews said. "I'll send him a card."

"That'd be thoughtful," Stuarti said. "Things like that mean a lot to oldsters."

Matthews smiled.

"You're a little tough to get hold of," Stuarti said. "Ninety-day compassionate leave, the guy tells me. Now as far as *I* remember, you're a little short on the bench in the family department. What happened? Your dog die?"

"I thought I'd take a little vacation," Matthews shrugged. "It'd been a while."

"At Mulready's Garage?" Stuarti demanded. "At least I think that's what the guy said when he answered the phone and said he'd take a message."

"Connecticut's garden garage," Matthews said. "Not everyone can go to Deauville on a civil service salary."

"Speaking of which," Stuarti said, "I understand there's some question of whether you're coming back at all. Harris in Personnel told me you'd filled out the disclosure permission forms to talk to outside employers. You thinking about getting a real live job?"

"I tried," Matthews smiled. "I even had interviews with a couple of the new consulting firms specializing in area studies and political risk analysis. One guy actually jabbered at me for half an hour about 'factor analysis of the capital investment climate in Yugoslavia' before I figured out that he was asking me if I knew who to bribe."

"No dummy there," Stuarti said. "What about the other one?"

"Global Econometrics, it was called," Matthews said. "The name should have tipped me off. The guy begins to read the education section of my resumé and immediately sniffs. 'A political scientist, eh?,' he says. 'Aren't you the people who believe that "data" is the plural of "anecdote"?' "

Stuarti giggled.

"Then he reads a little farther, says 'Holy shit!,' and asks me if I'm carrying a gun. I almost pissed on his desk."

"I'm afraid you're going to have to try harder if you expect to make it in the straight world," Stuarti said severely. "How did that thing for Domestic Operations go?"

"Interesting, actually," Matthews said easily. "More investigative accounting than anything else. I know a little more about putting a swerve on a balance sheet than I used to."

"That was what, guns?" Stuarti said.

"Yes," Matthews said. "A guy of ours, actually, who'd spent ten years buying and selling weapons in Clandestine Services Support before a couple of NORAID guys helped him figure out that going into business for himself, what with his contacts and all, might pay a little better than being a GS-twelve."

"Where does the investigative accounting come in?" Stuarti asked. "The IRA start issuing annual reports?"

" 'Humanitarian aid,' " Matthews said. "Nowadays, what with the administration talking about what a nice thing it is to do for the contras, or the mujaheddin, or whoever else they want to give a gun to this week, one tends to forget that the whole specious concept was invented by the IRA for North American fund-raising purposes. Holy Name Church's Las Vegas Night for the Children of Northern Ireland, Bingo for Peace, that kind of thing. Raise a quick forty grand and send the brave little tykes a Family-Pak of Hershey bars. Also a couple of crates of factory-packed AR-15 semis to sit on while they eat 'em. It was just a question of getting to the church's books."

"Which you did, I assume?" Stuarti asked mildly.

"Yes," Matthews said without elaboration. "The guy began doing his time down in Allenwood last month."

"That was quick," Stuarti said. "No attempt at graymail?"

"Sure," Matthews said. "In fact I was there when the guy's lawyer told the U.S. attorney, 'My client's not doing any time. Bring this thing to court,' he said, 'and the first thing I'm going to do is put my client on the stand and ask him if he's ever sold guns before. When my client says, yes, he has, I'm going to ask him when and where, and we'll spend two days reading the details into the court record. Of course, if that

57

prospect doesn't appeal to the Agency, well, my client's willing to forego his right to a trial in a court of law and plead this thing out. To jaywalking, say."

"Lippy bastard, sounds like," Stuarti said.

"Not for long," Matthews said. "I had a little chat with his client. Explained that while we understood that he had certain constitutionally guaranteed rights, there were rights on both sides. And that one of ours was to petition for denial of bond, which we'd do and which'd be upheld, and which would mean, given the time it takes to get on the federal docket, say, six months in Rikers waiting for trial. During which six months, I further pointed out, there was very little that we could do should some tough maniac with a knife somehow get the idea that he might be able to curry a little favor with the parole board by cutting off the guy's head and eating it. Told him that if I had to choose between six months at CIM Rikers, with his prospects, and six years at Allenwood, two to be served, that I'd start thinking about picking up an Oral B-40 and a little light reading, keep my goddamned mouth shut, and do my time."

There was a harsh and unfamiliar edge to Matthews's voice as he spoke, and for the first time Stuarti remarked the light and constant tremor of his hands.

"Clarity always helps," Stuarti observed.

"It did in this case, too," Matthews agreed, grimacing slightly. "The little shitbird changed his plea the next morning."

"Perhaps," Stuarti said uneasily, "I should fill you in a bit more fully than I've felt able to on the phone."

"Sure," Matthews said, straightening for a moment and changing his posture on the bed.

"Code-name Bunny," Stuarti began, folding his pudgy fingers across his paunch and assuming his pedagogic voice, "is a senior civilian EDP consultant to the Arms Control and Disarmament Agency. Circumstantial evidence, inadequate for prosecution but more than adequate for our purposes, indicates that for at least the past ten months code-name Bunny has been functioning as a Soviet asset, passing whatever he can get his hands on to a Bloc contact as yet unidentified.

"This evidence, as you know, was brought to our attention by Dr. Walter Butterfield—the ACDA guy I alluded to on the phone—who was his immediate superior. At our suggestion, and making it clear that he had not broached the subject elsewhere, Dr. Butterfield brought the possibility of a departmental leak to Bunny's attention. The thinking at the time, I believe, was to start him running and to watch where he went. It seems, however, that they decided to protect him rather than to pull him. You know the result."

"Yes," Matthews said, "two dead bodies." Reaching over, he lifted several books from the stack nearest Stuarti. The titles that came to his hand were Thomas Schelling's *The Strategy of Conflict*, Lawrence Freedman's *The Evolution of Nuclear Strategy*, and Bernard Brodie's *Escalation and the Nuclear Option*.

"Interesting reading list, Mary," Matthews said. "A new interest, or just rounding out your education?"

"Well," Stuarti said, "when your president comes right out and confesses with a winsome smile that he and some of his buddies are amateur Armageddon buffs, I figure it's probably a good idea to keep up."

"We know that code-name Bunny is a bad apple," Matthews said, almost to himself, "and yet he's still on the street, and you're willing to tell the Bureau whatever you have to to keep him there. Sounds like maybe you've got some plans for him."

"We do," Stuarti said flatly. "In point of fact, we've been ready and waiting for something like this for almost two years. Problem is, counterespionage cases on American soil are statutorily the Bureau's, and they *had* to be told. They currently have Bunny spiked every way from Sunday and have pavement teams on him twenty-four hours a day. It won't be long until they make his cutout, and when they do they'll grab him. We've gotta get there first."

"You're going to load him," Matthews said softly.

"Right to the goddamned gills," Stuarti said.

"With antique nuclear weapons policy?" Matthews said.

"That's the thing about nuclear weapons," Stuarti replied lightly. "You can't use 'em, might blow the place up. About all you *can* do is talk about them."

"How are you going to do the loading? Through the ACDA?"

"No," Stuarti said, settling back in the wheelchair and sighing with rich contentment. "It's going to be a full-fledged Big Store. First one I've run on this scale since the sixties. Enough to make a man feel young again."

"I assume you've already got your people lined up, then?" Matthews asked.

"The varsity," Stuarti said with simple pride. "Irving the Office Manager is supervising document production and technical details, Eliot the Casting Director is handling personnel in Washington, and yours truly has full responsibility for script and direction."

"Where does this Fifteenth of June Group fit in?" Matthews asked. "I'm not sure I understand your continuing interest."

"As I told you on the phone yesterday," Stuarti said, "the Bureau confirmed our suspicion that they've made themselves a mean new friend. The analysts have what they think is an East German accent on tape, and we're assuming HVA. We need the guy, Tom, and we need him yesterday."

"Why?" Matthews asked. "It would seem as though his role in things is already over."

"I suppose so," Stuarti sighed. "But the public perception of the risks posed by espionage is sometimes a bit fuzzy. Start talking to people about the reduction of radar signatures and hypothetical encryption of telemetry data and they're liable to go to sleep. Ask Minihan, our Bureau liaison to the IG.

60

On the other hand, *everybody* understands about nasty Germans, assassinated professors, and murdered little girls . . ."

"I see," Matthews said after a pause, and though his voice was mild the pale blue eyes behind his glasses held Stuarti in a steady gaze. "You might want to watch how you phrase that thought in the future, Mary. As it is, it almost sounded as though you just said that Dr. Butterfield had his head blown off in order to dress up a headline."

"You've probably got two weeks, tops," Stuarti said, ignoring Matthews's remark and shifting pronouns as smoothly as a Formula One driver gearing down for a curve. Bending from his chair, Stuarti picked up a blue plastic looseleaf notebook bearing a green security cover sheet and handed it to Matthews. "Summary log of the tap on Weinstein's phone," he said. "The second flag's the conversation I told you about."

When he had finished reading, Matthews handed the book back to Stuarti.

"Have we got a last name for this Jack?" he asked.

"Norris," Stuarti said. "He was released from Green Haven six months ago after doing two of five for selling guns. The guy's about your age and, no offense, dear boy, not a bad look-alike. Think you could be a gun dealer who failed to seize his opportunity to adjust to society? It'll check out if they bother."

"Sure," Matthews said.

"Congratulations," Stuarti said, handing Matthews a worn leather wallet. "You've also got a job in a gym on West Twelfth Street, starting tomorrow. It was arranged by your parole officer, whose card's in the wallet. It pays minimum wage, and you don't need to act a whole lot happier about it than the real guy would be. Is there anything you need that you don't have?"

"No," said Matthews softly, and Stuarti was conscious of a slight chill as his eyes flickered almost involuntarily to the small gym bag at Matthews's feet.

"Quite sure you've been all right, dear boy?" Stuarti asked. "You look like you've lost a little weight."

"Do I always contact you through the number here?" Matthews asked, standing.

"Twenty-four hours a day," Stuarti said. "If for some reason I'm not here they'll patch you through."

"I'll be in touch," Matthews said from the door, without turning.

"And I'll be waiting," Stuarti said gently. "Mind how you go, dear boy."

For several minutes after Matthews had left, Stuarti sat slumped in the wheelchair, his face thoughtful. At last he reached out, lifted the receiver from the gray scrambler phone, and pushed a button.

"It's Stuarti," he said when the phone was answered and the necessary buttons pushed. "Let me speak to Bullard."

Stuarti listened for a moment, drumming his fingers.

"Yes," he said, "you can. Got a pencil? Good. Tell him when he flies up tomorrow to bring a current copy of Tom Matthews's two-oh-one, plus the case file on whatever he was working on for Domestic. Yes, that's right. Tell him Security Matthews, he'll know."

Replacing the receiver, Stuarti wheeled himself slowly to the television, and when at last his Mormon knocked and entered the room, Stuarti was absorbed in "Mr. Rogers's Neighborhood" and did not wish to be disturbed.

CHAPTER NINE

THE unnatural pallor of Tom Matthews's skin, a diffidence in his address easily mistakable for a habit of deference, and the fact that both the security deposit and the first month's rent had been paid in cash were telltale signs to the superintendent of the tenement building on Sullivan Street north of Houston, where Matthews had that morning taken a room.

When Matthews moved in that afternoon, arriving on foot with nothing more than a superannuated blue lady's Samsonite suitcase bound with twine, a gym bag, and two cheap wool army blankets loosely wrapped in brown paper, suspicion became certainty, causing the super to regret the relative courtesy that, in his capacity as rental agent, he had that morning shown Matthews.

It was, therefore, in a tone that sought to redress his earlier magnanimity that the super addressed Matthews from the permanently half-open door of his ground floor apartment as Matthews, having by making his bed completed his move, descended the stairs to the street.

"Hey, you!" he called, risking the pronoun and winning, as Matthews obediently stopped and turned. "I wanna talk to you."

"Sure," Matthews said quietly.

Emboldened by his success, the super stepped from his apartment into the hall and pulled the door very nearly shut behind him, as though to indicate that it was his habit, as became a man, to spare his wife the hard facts of a harder world.

"Is that all your stuff?" the super demanded.

"Yes," Matthews said.

Sucking his teeth, the super looked Matthews insolently up and down, permitting him time to apologize for the paucity of his worldly goods. When Matthews failed to do so, the super felt himself obliged to speak candidly.

"Lissen'a me, pal," he said, "I seen guys like you before, and I got a pretty goddamn good idea where you been. Now I don't like niggers, I don't like faggots, *and I don't like cons*, so I'm only gonna tell you once. I don't put up with shit in my building, and you give me any trouble, well, I know your name and I got a dime, you unnerstan' me?"

"Sure," Matthews said, turning to leave.

"*No* cookin' inna' room, *no* hookers, and *no* TV after eleven. You got that, pal?"

"Yes," Matthews said without looking back, and he was gone.

"Good," said the super to the street door. "An' don't fuckin' forget it."

Reentering his apartment to applause from the television, the superintendent poured himself a victory shot of Four Roses from the bottle next to his chair.

"What was that?" demanded his wife from the Barca-lounger, not removing her eyes from the screen.

"Three-R," the super said. "Fuckin' guy musta thought I was blind or somethin'. Hadda straighten him out. You want one?"

The rich variousness and animated vitality of city streets seemed newly exotic to Matthews after his weeks in the country. As he strolled on Bleecker toward Sixth Avenue, he was pleasantly conscious of the chemical air, fragrant with roasting coffee and gasoline. Crossing the avenue and turning into Cornelia Street, he passed the exhaust fan of an Italian bakery, and if the intoxicating yeasty odors in which he was momentarily enveloped occasioned in him no hunger, neither did they cause the spasm of nausea that he expected. He was pleased, too, that his back caused him no discomfort as he walked, and that the constant stitch in his left side was barely noticeable.

It was as he reached the corner of West Fourth Street, satisfied with his ongoing progress report, that Matthews suddenly became aware of a faint whirring sound on the sidewalk behind him. Simultaneously a dark shape loomed in the corner of his peripheral vision, rapidly bearing down on him from behind in nearly utter silence.

Matthews moved with startling speed for a large man, and by the time the black teenager on the ten-speed bike belatedly blew his whistle and flashed by, he was well off the sidewalk, crouched, legs tensed, between two parked cars.

For a frozen moment Matthews remained motionless, then straightened slowly, his breathing ragged, his progress report revised, and the stitch in his left side throbbing like a broken tooth.

With a mocking wave the bicyclist swerved into Sixth Avenue traffic and was gone, and thus only the proprietor of the Pink Poodle erotic toy store across the street ever saw the gun, toylike in Matthews's broad flat hand, as he replaced it beneath his poplin windbreaker and resumed walking up West Fourth Street toward Sheridan Square, his pale hunter's face impassive and his left elbow held closely to his side.

It was two minutes past three when the man entered the Club Fifty-one on Sheridan Square, and Matthews guessed that he had arrived early and had been killing time outside.

Perhaps thirty years old, the man was handsome, almost

pretty. His head was leonine, bushy with dark curls, and far too large for his shoulders. He wore a calfskin jacket and Dior sunglasses pushed up into the curls. Even without *The New York Times* he carried, he would have looked out of place in the Club Fifty-one.

The bartender was a thin white man with thin gray hair combed straight back. He wore a stained white shirt two sizes too large and an apron folded at the waist. The TV was tuned to "The 700 Club," loud, to discourage conversation.

"What's yours?" he said to the man, his eyes still on the TV, where a black man in a suit and a famous baseball player were praising the Lord in tandem for His wisdom in having delivered RBIs in three figures in the player's option year.

"Let me have a draft Guinness," the pretty man said, swinging his leg over a cracked red vinyl banquette and settling onto it as though it were a saddle. "Cold mug, if you've got one, and a nice head."

"I think maybe you've got the wrong bar, sonny," the bartender said, still watching TV. "That's next door, there, where you get the Guinness and the head."

"How about a St. Pauli Girl?"

"What?"

Standing, Matthews pocketed a five-dollar bill, leaving a one and change on the bar.

"Thanks," he said to the bartender.

"Anytime," the bartender said.

Matthews turned to the pretty man. "Is that *The Times*?"

"Yes," the man said carefully, his face tensing. "You want to see it?"

"No," Matthews said. "It was just so I'd know who you were, is all. Let's take a walk."

Emerging onto Christopher Street from the artificial night of the bar, the men turned left, then left again onto Waverly Place. It was the pretty man who spoke first.

"Hey, listen, you're the, you're Vinnie's guy, right?"

"I'm not Vinnie's anything," Matthews said. "You Mark?"

"Yeah," the man said. "You wanna tell me where we're goin'?"

"Sure," Matthews said. "We're going for a walk around the block, talk a little, see if maybe we can do some business."

"What maybe?" the man asked as they swung right by a laundromat, heading toward Greenwich Avenue. "When we talked on Tuesday you said you were gonna have something for me. Today."

"I also told you," Matthews said, "that guys who're in a big hurry for a piece make me nervous. I told you that, didn't I?"

"Yeah," Weinstein said, "and I . . ."

"Sellin' guns," Matthews said. "It's kinda' like Cops and Robbers, you know what I mean?"

"No," Weinstein said.

"Sure," Matthews said. "You don't want to sell one to a cop, and you don't want to sell one to a robber. Either of 'em can get you in the shit, double quick. Stand right here for a minute and look like you're in love."

Smiling into Weinstein's eyes and ignoring the passersby, Matthews ran his hand slowly over Weinstein's chest and stomach, then up under his jacket, beneath the arms.

"Hey . . ." Weinstein began.

"Relax," Matthews said. "Seein' a couple of guys groping each other around here's about as rare as seein' a pigeon, you know what I mean? No big deal."

"I don't need this," the man said.

"No wire," Matthews said with satisfaction. "Now all you gotta do is promise me you're not a bad guy and maybe we can do some business."

"I'm not a bad guy," Weinstein said sullenly, following Matthews onto Greenwich Avenue.

"I could tell," Matthews said, smiling. "You know the Beretta model Eighty-four?"

"No," Weinstein said, brightening.

"Very nice," Matthews said. "It's a .380 auto, takes thirteen

67

rounds, 9 mm. short. Double action, semiautomatic, positive coil spring extractor, and a staggered magazine. It goes where you point it, and it doesn't jam. I think you'll like it."

"How much?" Weinstein asked.

"Three and a quarter," Matthews said. "Costs two thirty-five in the store."

"Good," Weinstein said without hesitation. "Where do we do this?"

"Suit yourself," Matthews shrugged. "The price includes delivery. Say, tomorrow night, around eight o'clock. You pick the place."

"What's this 'tomorrow' shit?" the pretty man said, his face reddening. "That's what I came here for today, was to buy a gun . . ."

"And that's what you're doing," Matthews said. "Look, I don't even know you, so it's nothing personal, you understand? It's not like I'm asking you to front it or something. You want to go down to Washington Square, there, ask around, you can probably find something before dinner. Cheaper, too. 'Course the thing's likely to blow up in your hand the first time you test-fire it, or else you find out about the unbalanced cylinder for the first time when you're standing there dry-snapping the fucking thing. Me, if I was you and actually thought I might need something, I'd go for the quality and save money on something else. Tomorrow night's when I'll have the piece, so that's when you can have it. You want it?"

"Shit," Weinstein said heavily. "Yeah, I want it."

"Where?"

"I'm gonna be visiting a friend," Weinstein said after a moment of hesitation. "Three-twelve West Nineteenth. Ring the buzzer for Weinstein. Say eight or a little after."

Matthews said nothing as he nodded, turned, and left.

At a magazine kiosk next to the Waverly Theater Matthews bought that morning's *New York Post* and a copy of *The Economist*. Taking these with him into the Blarney Stone bar next to Emilio's Italian restaurant, Matthews spent the next forty-five minutes at the end of the bar nearest the street window nursing two draft beers and reading *The Economist*. Leaving the bar—and the magazine—at four-thirty, he strolled a block south to Carmine Street where, from a public telephone, the *Post* folded open to the classifieds on the shelf before him, he made his call.

The phone was answered on the first ring.

"Let me talk to Stuarti," Matthews said.

"I'm sorry," said an unctuous voice at the other end of the line, "but there's no one here by that name. May I take a message?"

"No," Matthews said. "Just put him on the phone."

There was an extended pause. In the background Matthews could hear whispering, and then the sound of aluminum struts clashing against wood, as though someone had dropped a lawn chair.

"Goddamned things," wheezed Stuarti, breathing hard. "Tom?"

"Yes," Matthews said. "Who the hell was that?"

"Irving the Office Manager," Stuarti said, "and I think that you hurt his feelings."

"Does he always take messages from wrong numbers?"

"He gets a little overexcited in the field," Stuarti said, "but he's doing a dandy job for us, and we're all proud. Did Weinstein show?"

"Yes," Matthews said. "And the guy is scared to death."

"I should imagine so," Stuarti said. "He doesn't have to be a Leibniz to figure out that he's gotten in a little over his head. How did you leave it?"

"His place, tomorrow night," Matthews said. "He told me he was visiting a friend named Weinstein."

"A regular Moriarty, the guy," Stuarti laughed. "Reminds me of Arthur's favorite party game, Antimasquerade. Where the object's to go to a party disguised as yourself and successfully avoid recognition."

"Weinstein's where we start," Matthews said. "If your guy's ready, I can't see any point in waiting."

"Me neither," Stuarti said. "Did I tell you we were using Harold Baines for this?"

"The contract guy you flew all the way to Vienna just to throw up on a mailman?" Matthews asked. "That Harold?"

"That's him," Stuarti said proudly. "Harold-Who-Does-the-Disgusting-Things. He's about forty-five, dark hair, glasses. He'll be carrying a mop and a pail and, if I know Harold, he'll be overacting. I promised him I'd ask you to be sure not to get carried away and kick him in the nuts or anything by mistake."

"Tell him not to worry," Matthews said.

"Do you know yet what your backup requirements will be?" Stuarti asked. "The Bureau's promised us whatever we need in the way of cars and bodies."

"A car and a driver and another guy ought to do it," Matthews said, "but nobody moves until I call, *compris*? I don't want anybody behind me."

Again Stuarti discerned the hard and unfamiliar edge to Matthews's voice, whether of fear, or fatigue, or anger, he could not tell.

"Absolutely, dear boy," he said soothingly. "Nobody moves until you say so. Have you everything you need?"

"Yes," Matthews said.

"And you're sure you're quite all right, dear boy?" Stuarti asked. "You sound a little . . ."

But by then the line was dead.

It was dusk when Matthews returned to his rented room, carrying in a cardboard box beneath his arm orange juice, peanut butter, bread, Sanka, and a single setting of cheap china purchased from a sidewalk vendor on Houston Street.

The superintendent, for whom the satisfying memory of their earlier interview was still clearly warm, watched from the doorway of his apartment, face darkening, as Matthews approached the base of the stairs.

70

"What are you, deaf?" he demanded as Matthews drew abreast. "I thought I told you no cookin' inna—"

Here both the sentence and the super's hopes for a second helping of self-regard at Matthews's expense ended abruptly as, catching the man by the throat with his free hand, Matthews plucked him from the doorway of his apartment as effortlessly as one might remove a cork from a bottle.

"There's some loose change in my shirt pocket," Matthews said quietly. "Take it out."

Fumbling, for his hands were shaking badly and his vision blurred, the super complied. Forty-two cents.

"Take twelve cents," Matthews said.

The super did so.

"Now you've got everything you need if you decide to drop a dime on me, you little shitbird," Matthews said. "Ten cents for the phone company, and the pennies for your eyes, after. If I were you I'd think twice."

As best he could without speech, the super managed to convey the heartfelt impression that, after reconsideration, he, too, would think twice before taking such a precipitate step.

Matthews, never having put down his box of groceries, left him gagging on the stairs.

At 7:15 Matthews had his supper; half a quart of orange juice and a peanut butter sandwich, which he ate rapidly.

At 8:15 he brushed his teeth, turned down his bed, and dissolving a packet of hibitane in the sink prepared the compresses that he knew he would need that night.

At 8:30 he extinguished the room's single bulb and lay quietly on his cot, where, with practiced patience, he did to death the hours 'til dawn, dreaming only once, at the edge of sleep, of a dark-haired woman with cornflower eyes who waited in a cottage on a wooded hill.

71

CHAPTER TEN

T. HARRISON Bullard, wearing a three-piece Dunhill and an expression of pinched disapproval, stood among the packing crates in the living room of the Thirteenth Street townhouse watching censoriously as Stuarti, resplendent in a shiny new wheelchair and a paisley dressing gown, rummaged greedily through the briefcase of papers that Bullard had brought, pausing only occasionally to make a notation on the clipboard in his lap.

When Stuarti showed no signs of looking up, Bullard sniffed twice, announcing his intention to speak.

"You need a Kleenex?" Stuarti asked, scribbling.

"I must tell you," Bullard began formally, "that I had told Blaine, even before I knew about the wheelchair, that I could think of no one less appropriate than you to assume command responsibility for an operation of this magnitude."

"Ton cul," Stuarti said without looking up.

"There's no need to thank me," Bullard said stiffly, "or to be sarcastic, if that's what you're being. Our business requires both stern judgment and unflinching candor."

"You must be thinking of family planning," Stuarti said. "Our business *abominates* candor."

"Do you mind?" shuddered Bullard. "Is simple civility too much to . . ."

"*Far* too much," Stuarti said. "Irving was up yesterday, and brought me up to date on the technical stuff. What does Eliot have to report? Has he finished casting?"

"Pretty much," Bullard said sulkily. "He's still looking for a chief of Naval Operations, but he's had the rest of them in eight-hour-a-day rehearsal for the past ten days. He says they're coming along nicely, and should be ready for the site rehearsal by the end of next week. Speaking of which, Blaine's secured office space in the Old Executive Office building for an entity called the Southwest Asian Working Group. A lobby area, two offices, and small and large conference rooms on the third floor. Eliot's seen it and reports himself satisfied."

"Good," Stuarti said, a file folder open on his lap. "This polygraph transcript's dated fourteen months ago. Is that the last time Matthews was fluttered?"

"Yes," Bullard said. "He was due the second week of January, but took three months off starting the first of the year. Compassionate leave, the letter said. Normally the flutter date gets pushed up if there's a scheduling conflict, but then those I-6 Security guys don't always seem to be subject to the normal rules. I guess nobody wants to be the one to tell a state-of-the-art Doberman that he's eating out of the wrong dish."

"Whose crack is that?" Stuarti snapped, prepared to be genuinely angry. "Just another bon mot from the Lhasa apso set?"

"Everybody's," shrugged Bullard, "nobody's. Those guys are thugs, and so is Matthews. His languages and the degrees don't change that, they just make it creepier."

"Matthews isn't a thug," Stuarti said, his tone again even.

"His career ladder *is* an odd one, I'll grant you that," Bullard said. "Why would someone ever transfer out of Analysis and Estimate to Operations, much less out of Operations to I-6 Security? Surely you'll admit that's a bit peculiar."

"Is it?" Stuarti asked. "Nice and straightforward, security work. No nagging ambiguities. I can see where a tired man might find that attractive."

"Attractive?" For a moment Bullard stared at Stuarti, appalled, then his face relaxed.

"Of course," he said, wagging a reproving finger. "I forgot. You *know* Matthews. Knew him when he was in Operations, didn't you?"

"I knew him in Paris when he was first in Operations, and we once spent a week together in Hamburg waiting for a Pole of his to come out," Stuarti said, his eyes momentarily distant. "Yes, I know him."

"What happened to the Pole?" demanded Bullard, whose ear was excellent, but Stuarti had no time, just then, for reminiscence.

"Did you bring the case file on that thing Matthews was working on for domestic?" Stuarti asked, bending again to his papers.

"Yes," Bullard said.

"Did you read it?"

"Of course."

"Refresh my memory," Stuarti said. "It's been a while."

"It was a moonlighter," Bullard said wearily, extending his pudgy fingers and admiring his signet ring. "A guy in CS Support who decided to go into business for himself with NORAID as a client. They were using a church up near Isham Park in Manhattan to launder the funds. Matthews made friends with an Irish schoolteacher named O'Kearney they had helping out with the books. Almost lost her, too."

"What do you mean?" Stuarti asked.

"Apparently the U.S. attorney decided that they needed a few more pictures than they had," Bullard said, wandering to the window and peering out. "They had to send Matthews's girl back for a second bite. This time she got caught. And got her hands slammed in a car door a few times to convince her that testifying was a bad idea."

74

"Did she testify?" Stuarti asked quietly.

"Didn't have to," Bullard said, turning from the window. "The guy decided to plead it at the last minute. After a two-minute chat with Matthews while his lawyer was out of the room. The lawyer apparently went nuts, screaming that Matthews had threatened his client, but the guy had seen the light, I guess, and that was that. No report of threats, no complaints, and a flat plea to the original charges. Good thing we know that Matthews isn't a thug, or Lord knows what we might think."

"What happened to the O'Kearney woman?" Stuarti asked.

"The record's not entirely clear," Bullard said. "She sort of disappears into the mist of ancillary files. 'Reference by permission to Personalities Annex,' 'Inquiries to Federal Marshal Service,' that sort of thing. Federal Witness Protection Program, I assume. What difference does it make? The guy plead the thing."

"None," Stuarti agreed cheerfully, and it was only when Bullard began to speak again that he glanced at his watch and noticed the time.

"Christ!" he exclaimed. "I'm never gonna make it! I have to be dressed by ten, and it's twenty-five till."

"May I help you?" Bullard asked, with an understanding glance at Stuarti's wheelchair.

"Help me what?" Stuarti said sharply.

"Get dressed," said Bullard with shy pride. "My dad was in a wheelchair at the end. I know what I'm doing."

"Why not?" shrugged Stuarti.

"Let's just get you onto the bed first, shall we?" Bullard said in a brisk nurse's voice, kneeling and locking the wheels of Stuarti's chair.

"How can I say no?" Stuarti said.

"Just put your arms around my neck," Bullard said, passing his arms beneath Stuarti's and bracing his legs.

"Be gentle," murmured Stuarti, wrapping his arms around Bullard's neck and drawing his head down onto his shoulder.

75

"On three," Bullard said, his voice muffled in Stuarti's dressing gown. "One, two . . ."

"You smell like gardenias," whispered Stuarti, rubbing his nose against Bullard's cheek.

"Cut it out!" Bullard said sharply, as together they lurched to their feet, Stuarti hanging from his neck.

"I love you," breathed Stuarti, nipping at Bullard's ear.

"Stop it! Stop it!" cried Bullard. "You filthy pervert!"

"No offense, Bullard," Stuarti said, pushing him away and shuffling over to the window to peer out, "but your bedside manner sucks."

"You can walk!" cried Bullard accusingly.

"Of course," Stuarti said, turning and regarding him with a puzzled frown. "That's why God gave us legs. Has Blaine pitched Dr. Doom yet?"

"I presume," Bullard said after a censorious pause, "that your inappropriate reference is to Professor Quade."

"That's the one," Stuarti said, "the Arms Control guy. Has Blaine talked to him yet?"

"Yes," Bullard said icily.

"What'd he say?"

"He had some initial reservations," Bullard said, "but Blaine is a very persuasive man."

"Good," Stuarti said. "We could have used someone else in a pinch, but we know that Bunny's heard him speak before, and that should help."

"Anything else?" Bullard asked stiffly, putting on his overcoat.

"Yes," Stuarti said. "Tell Blaine we're taking Weinstein tonight. And tell him I'm going to use Harold-Who-Does-the-Disgusting-Things. Blaine always liked Harold."

"Harold isn't the only one," Bullard said coldly.

"You're cute when you pout, Bullard," Stuarti said, pursing his lips and blowing him a kiss. "Have a nice flight."

* * *

As always in the last hours before action involving his operatives, Stuarti was uneasy, restless. After allowing Irving the Office Manager, in a call frantic with excitement and factitious urgency, to persuade him to request the use of a diplomatic pouch for transport of an East German type font, Stuarti dismissed his Mormon and sat alone by the window in the dying light of the afternoon, rereading the files that Bullard had brought and brooding.

It was very nearly dark, Minihan's arrival with the day's transcripts imminent, when Stuarti picked up the receiver and opened the line on the scrambler phone.

"We'll go over on three," said a tinny voice slowly. "One, two . . ."

Stuarti depressed another button.

"Two things," he said. "First, I need to talk to an inmate at FCF Allenwood. That's right, Club Fed, there. Have the warden arrange it, and then patch it back to me through Langley. Second, I need a name traced through from an Operations file annex . . ." Stuarti paused, listened. "Absolutely," he said. "If not sooner. Got a pencil?"

CHAPTER ELEVEN

HAROLD Baines, like Stuarti, was always nervous on the eve of a performance. Though in youth he had been hailed as "a compelling Coriolanus," "a memorable Macduff," the passing of years and the exigencies of family life had recast him more nearly to type, condemning him to play Willy Loman in perpetuity as a salesman for a manufacturer of medical supplies.

Where others found the discounting of bedpans and prostheses inadequate as the stuff of tragedy, Harold did not. For Harold, his life was a nearly unrelieved blackness, illuminated only by secret nights such as the one before him, when the moon was full, his country called, and again as Terror and Pity he strode the boards.

Alone, then, in the bathroom of the family brick bungalow, one of countless such in the galactic wastes between Manhattan and LaGuardia Airport, Harold stood, exalted, before the mirror, and began to bring himself to focus.

Wearing only his sleeveless undershirt and boxer shorts, Harold removed his glasses and, leaning forward, began carefully to examine the shape of his face. The examination completed, he stripped the foil from one of several condoms that sat on the edge of the sink and carefully half-filled the diaphanous tube with water from the tap. Tying it off as one would a water balloon, he inserted the condom between his cheek and gum and again leaned to the mirror, prodding critically. Satisfied, he straightened and regarded himself stonily, his eyes without mercy. Then, suddenly and without warning casting aside an imaginary mop, he shouted, "Freeze, you son of a bitch!" reaching, as he did so, for an equally imaginary gun at his hip.

Poor Harold never cleared leather.

Instead, struck somehow in the chest, he reeled backward, eyes widening, water pouring from his mouth and nostrils as he bit down on the condom.

Having supposed himself alone in the house, Harold's involuntary scream of terror was very nearly as loud as that of his wife, who, rooted in the doorway, hand at her throat, regarded him with bulging eyes.

"What's the matter?! Whatta ya doing?! Who're ya talkin to?!"

"I thought you were out," Harold panted, wondering briefly if his hair was actually standing on end.

"I *was* out," Harold's wife said, "Now I'm back in. Why're ya' screamin? Why're ya blowin water outta your nose?"

"Never mind," Harold said stiffly, attempting to remove the condom unobtrusively from his mouth.

Alas, unobtrusively removing a used condom from his mouth under the hostile scrutiny of his wife proved a task beyond even Harold's considerable gifts.

"What's that?" she demanded. "Lemme . . ." Struck suddenly silent with horror and recognition, Harold's wife recoiled, her face a mask of repugnance. "Oh, *my God!*"

"It's a prop," Harold said, in an utterly bootless attempt at dignity.

"Prop, my ass," Harold's wife snarled, regarding him as though his eyelashes were crawling with pin worms. "It's a *rubber*. In your *mouth*. You ever do this sorta sick shit in front of the kids and I'll have you in jail, you pervert!"

His composure returning, Harold addressed his wife in a tone of gentle pity, his face filled with quiet pride and the glow of a love that dares not speak its name; like a man, say, having an affair of the heart with an inflatable doll.

"I don't expect you to understand," he said archly. "All I can tell you is that it involves national security."

"My mother told me," she said, processing and dismissing Harold's ludicrous claim with lightning speed, "that there were twisted geeks out there who got their cookies by doin' stuff like standin' around in their undies and blowin' water outta their noses with a rubber in their mouth. I didn't believe her. I thought she was fuckin' *nuts*. I was wrong."

Shaking her head, she turned on her heel and left.

It was with a certain glumness vis-à-vis the coming days, therefore, that Harold completed his toilet; donning work clothes and a tattered gray cardigan, filling the remaining condoms with water and food dye, and fetching from the utility closet an aluminum bucket and a mop.

On his way out, he paused in the living room, put down his mop and pail, and addressed the back of his wife's head, which was watching "Live at Five" and sucking on a tall Bud.

"I'm going out," he said.

"Thanks," she said without turning. "I'll call the neighbors, tell 'em to get the kids in."

"I may be late," he said.

"Not late enough," she said.

Harold was halfway down the front walk, thus, trudging to his rendezvous with destiny like a laid-off laborer lugging his lunch pail home, when his inamorata called from the front door.

"Hey, Kissinger," she yelled. "Ya forgot your national security mop."

The apartment in which Mark Weinstein lived—and from which he conducted his small-time drug business—overlooked

Nineteenth Street west of Eighth Avenue from the fourth floor of a decaying brownstone. The stoop of the building was empty, the weather being unseasonably raw, and from a head shop on the corner of Eight Avenue—in previous months a laundromat and a pizzeria as it passed inexorably through the phases of its metamorphosis to Chinese restaurant—Matthews could discern a glow of light in the windows against the evening gloom.

Obtaining change from the clerk, Matthews phoned from a public telephone booth on the corner that, despite the fact that its glass sides had long ago been kicked in, still smarted sharply with the odor of stale urine.

Weinstein answered on the second ring.

"Yes?" he said.

"How the hell am I supposed to get in?" demanded Matthews.

There was a pause.

"Is this Jack?" asked Weinstein, his voice confused.

"You said after eight," Matthews said. "It's almost eight-thirty. How do I get in?"

"Ring the buzzer," Weinstein said, "Four-A."

"The thing's broken," Matthews said. "I tried."

"Are you sure?" Weinstein said, and from the delay in his response Matthews, with satisfaction, assumed him to be stoned.

"Absolutely," Matthews said, not bothering to add that from across the street, ten minutes earlier, he had watched Harold pry the intercom unit from the wall and leave it dangling from its wires. "Are we just gonna chat on the phone, here, or are we going to do some business?"

"Yes," Weinstein said, "yes. I'll come down."

"And you're alone, right?" Matthews said. "I don't want to make any new friends."

"Yes," Weinstein said again.

"Make it quick," said Matthews.

Weinstein had already descended the stairs by the time Matthews arrived and was holding the inside door open, glumly regarding the wreckage of the intercom panel.

"It doesn't work," Matthews said. "I tried it."

"Fuckin' junkies," Weinstein said, shaking his head in disgust and foggily wondering which of his customers could possibly have been that handy with tools.

"Is that it?" Matthews said. "Seems like there're more guys runnin' around loose here, that *should* be in jail, than there *were* in jail."

Weinstein raised his eyes from the tangle of wires and attempted to focus on Matthews.

"You were in jail?" he asked.

"Yeah," said Matthews, "Green Haven."

"No shit," said Weinstein, brightening. "What for?"

"Selling guns," Matthews said shortly. "Which, if you maybe remember, is why I'm here."

"Yeah, right," Weinstein said, coloring. "C'mon in, and be careful you don't break your neck. They're washing the floors, and the steps are slippery as hell."

The door to the vestibule had barely closed behind them when the clanking of an aluminum bucket and the low murmur of sullen curses announced the author of the newly wet steps. As Weinstein and Matthews watched, Harold emerged from the base of the stairwell, roughly shoving his bucket before him with his foot and occasionally swiping at the water that slopped onto the floor with a chillingly authentic indifference.

Glancing disinterestedly at them, Harold began to bend again to the bucket when suddenly he froze, his eyes flashing upward to fix Weinstein with a sudden shock of recognition.

What happened next, it seemed to Weinstein, happened with a speed outside of time. Kicking the bucket away with a shattering clatter and hurling his mop behind him, Harold screamed, "U.S. Treasury Department! Freeze, you son of a bitch!" grappling as he did so for the plastic military .45-

caliber automatic ($4.99 at Toys "Я" Us) beneath the cardigan at his waist.

It was the sweater, Weinstein saw quite clearly from the floor where Matthews had shoved him, that proved Harold's undoing, for in the instant that Harold's .45 tangled in the cardigan, a gun blossomed, as if by magic, in Matthews's hand, rising until it was on a dead line with Harold's chest at point blank range.

In the narrow hallway the deafening sound of Matthews's shot seemed less a discharge than a detonation. Harold was hurled backward into a bank of mailboxes where, eyes widening and beginning to roll upward, he gurgled once the word "Mother . . ." (confirming Stuarti's suspicion of his propensity for overacting) before sliding abruptly to the floor, blood exploding from his mouth and nose.

Matthews jacked the empty round from the chamber, slipped the gun beneath his jacket, and bent, jerking Weinstein to his feet. Before the brass casing of the blank cartridge had ceased dancing on the linoleum floor they were on the street, strolling unhurriedly away toward Ninth Avenue, Matthews's arm draped in comradely fashion around Weinstein's shoulders, for control.

"Jesus Christ!" whispered Weinstein, his voice whistling in his teeth and his legs trembling, "Oh, Jesus Christ!"

"Shut up and listen," Matthews said evenly. "We need a bolt-hole, someplace we can go and stay 'til morning where we won't have to worry about the cops. Got a friend, might do that for us?"

"My God!" Weinstein whimpered again, his voice now beginning to climb, "you shot a cop!"

"That's right," Matthews said with the same chilling evenness, his arm drifting over Weinstein's shoulder and snugging up against his neck, "and after that everything's a freebie. Now either you've got someplace for us to go or I don't need you anymore, my friend. Which is it?"

For a dreadful moment Weinstein simply stared at Matthews, his face blank with shock, until Matthews gave a sharp tug on his hair and managed to get him started again.

"I know a place," Weinstein stammered. "I've got a friend in the East Village . . ."

"Good," said Matthews, signaling a cab.

In the block behind them harsh male voices began to shout, blue lights began to flash spectrally, and in the vestibule, forgiving himself the unscripted "Mother," Harold proudly awarded himself both ears and the tail.

CHAPTER TWELVE

A t Matthews's direction, the cab took them briefly across town to Union Square. There they caught a southbound IRT train one stop to St. Mark's Place. On the principle, perhaps, that the man with the gun is always the host, Matthews paid for the cab and provided Weinstein with a subway token. Otherwise he did not speak at all, offering neither threat nor comfort, and it was thus unclear to Weinstein, as they emerged from the underground in front of Cooper Union and began to walk south, precisely when he had ceased to be an accomplice and had become a prisoner.

The tenement building that proved to be their destination was on the south side of Sixth Street, just east of Avenue A. The building shared a basement with the corner bodega that it adjoined, and the hallway behind the unlocked front door was nearly blocked by stacks of empty cardboard boxes marked Goya. The master lock to the mailbox bank was missing, and on the wall above a torn and yellowing notice from the post office announced the suspension of delivery service. In the light of the single bulb that illuminated the hallway, Matthews could see, behind an open door at the end, the bare porcelain bowl of a communal toilet and wondered briefly about the logistics of fencing a toilet seat. Above the ubiquitous stench of urine, the smells were of garlic, stale cooking oil, steam, and decay.

Together they climbed the stairs, Weinstein leading. The walls were shedding their most recent coat of institutional aluminum paint in great leprous blisters, and the doors that they passed, two to a floor, were uniformly sheathed in sheet metal.

At the door of 3R, Weinstein knocked, paused, and knocked again. From behind the door, a woman's voice said sullenly, "Yeah?"

"It's Mark," Weinstein said.

There was the rattle of the bar of a police lock, the click of a dead bolt, and the door swung open, flooding the hallway with the sweet smell of marijuana.

The girl who stood before them was short and slim, with dark eyes and blond hair worn in pigtails. She was wearing denim overalls over a white T-shirt and was barefoot, and as they passed inside and the door closed behind them Matthews reflected that Priscilla No-Last-Name looked more like a farmer's daughter than a dangerous little girl with a strong taste for rough trade.

The apartment was a single room with a wooden counter separating a Pullman kitchenette from the living area. In one corner of the room a stained double mattress heaped with bedclothes and dirty laundry served as a sleeping pallet. A low couch, seat-sprung, threadbare, stood against the opposite wall, the only seating other than the bed. On the low yellow plastic coffee table before it a box from Ray's Famous Pizza, half filled with crusts and stubbed cigarette butts, rested on an untidy stack of old *New York Post*s. A cardboard shoe box on the table held at one end an ounce or so of cleaned grass and at the other the seeds and stems that had been winnowed from it with a playing card. Next to the grass there was a magnum of Remy Martin, three-fourths empty, and two glasses. The room's other appointments were Azuma-one-stop; a dusty shade of bamboo slats inadequately covering the steel gratings that shrouded the room's single window, and identical green rice paper fixtures with a dragon and pagoda motif dimming both the single standing lamp and the bare bulb hanging above the kitchenette. The room held neither books nor paintings nor photographs, and Matthews guessed that it was Priscilla No-Last-Name's habit not to stay in any one place too long.

Without speaking, Weinstein crossed to the table, poured three fingers of Cognac into a dirty glass, and tossed it off, shuddering. As he lit a cigarette, both Matthews and the girl watched the shaking of his hands without comment.

Turning to the girl, Weinstein began to speak, was forced to stop, breathe deeply, and begin again.

"Listen," he said to the girl, his voice tremulous, "we've got a problem . . ."

" 'We,' you and me," the girl asked dreamily, "or 'we,' you and your friend with no name here?"

"Jack," said Weinstein, "this's Jack. Works over at the Attic Gym."

"Hi, Jack," the girl said, turning to Matthews.

"Hi," Matthews said, smiling and pointing to a door off the kitchenette. "Is that the bathroom?"

"Yes," said the girl.

"Anybody in there?" Matthews asked, still smiling and not looking at the two glasses on the table.

"No," said the girl, "but we could probably get somebody, you like that sort of thing."

"For Christ's sake, Priscilla," Weinstein breathed. "Don't jerk the guy's chain! He's on fuckin' parole and he just blew away a goddamned cop in the lobby of my building!"

The girl licked her lips, her eyes suddenly brighter.

"Is that right?" she asked, directing her question to Weinstein but keeping her eyes on Matthews.

87

"Right in fuckin' half," Weinstein said, "blood all over the . . ."

"No," said Matthews from the now open bathroom door, turning and letting the girl see the handgun as he replaced it beneath his jacket. "The guy was a Treasury agent, not a cop."

"If he can bust you, he's a cop," Weinstein said sullenly, avoiding Matthews's eyes and pouring himself another drink.

"You know what Treasury agents do?" Matthews asked the girl, ignoring Weinstein.

"Funny money?" shrugged the girl, smiling and not taking her eyes from Matthews's.

"Alcohol, Tobacco, and Firearms," Matthews said. "They bust moonshiners, cigarette smugglers, and guys who sell guns. Like me. Of course they have to know where you're gonna be, with the gun and the guy who's gonna buy it, before they can do it."

"Hey . . ." said Weinstein.

"And they did, too," Matthews said.

"*Hey* . . ." Weinstein said, "Wait a . . ."

The blow with which Matthews struck Weinstein in the stomach folded him in half like a rag doll, lifting him sufficiently off the ground that the first thing to strike the floor was his head.

On the floor at Matthews's feet, Weinstein gasped and gagged, his feet scrabbling helplessly for purchase on the smooth wood.

"They should have told you," Matthews said quietly, looking down, "that it can be a tough way to earn a favor, something goes wrong. And letting you go downstairs alone was dumb."

Weinstein, his eyes and nose running, turned his face up to look at Matthews and gagged a word that Matthews could not understand.

"What did he say?" Matthews asked the girl.

"It sounded like 'bumps,' " she said, with an eager smile

88

that suggested to Matthews that she was either insane or on something a whole lot stronger than grass.

Weinstein shook his head, gagged, and tried again.

"Bombs!" he gasped.

"It was 'bombs!' " the girl said gaily, with the brightness of a winner at a party game.

"Go ahead," Matthews said to Weinstein.

"Bombs . . . Treasury Department . . . they do bombings . . . wasn't you . . ."

"I don't sell bombs," Matthews said.

"No," gasped Weinstein, "me, me . . ."

"He sells bombs?" Matthews asked the girl with open incredulity. "I didn't know *anybody* sells bombs."

"Mostly dope, I thought," the girl said, entering happily into the game. "At least he never *mentioned* any bombs."

"Priscilla, you cunt . . ." Weinstein wheezed, now openly weeping, "tell him . . . Andreas . . . the guy in Greenwich . . ."

The girl knelt and stroked Weinstein's face gently. Her voice, as she made her choice, was tender, as though she were addressing a child.

"Markie, honey," she said, "I've known you for a long time, right?"

Weinstein wept.

"Now I want you to do something for me, OK?"

Weinstein nodded helplessly.

"You gotta stop crying, Markie," she said, a smile beginning to play around her lips. "It's a little bit of a downer, honey, and I paid good money for this dope."

Weinstein stared at her for a moment, uncomprehending, and it was only when she began to giggle that he realized the finality with which she had cut him loose. He then screamed "No!" and grabbed wildly at the laughing girl, reaching for her hair, as Matthews, this time with genuine regret, struck him with the side of his foot, again in the stomach, putting an end to speech.

Matthews bound Weinstein hand and foot with strips of

torn sheet and gagged him with a wadded pair of panties that Priscilla offered from a heap of crumpled laundry in the corner.

Pointing Priscilla to the couch, on which she obediently sat, hands folded primly in her lap like a schoolgirl eager to please, Matthews then made his call, the mewing sounds from the floor beside him assuring him of Weinstein's attention.

Matthews dialed a number with a New Jersey area code. Stuarti's Mormon answered on the first ring.

"Lemme talk to Eddie S.," Matthews said. "No, I don't. Ask him when he gets off the phone." There was a pause. "Hello, Eddie," Matthews said as Stuarti growled hello. "Listen for a minute and you oughta recognize the . . . yeah, yeah. . . . Well, not bad. . . . No, Green Haven sucked, is what Green Haven did. Listen, I got a little problem . . ." Again there was a pause. "No," Matthews said, "as a matter of fact it's a guy, and I need a car and a couple of guys and another car, fairly fast . . . No, I only need the one car where I am, and I don't give a shit about the other as long's it's got a trunk. . . . That's right . . . Manhattan. Sixth Street, two buildings east of Avenue A. . . . No, I think maybe morning, when there're a few more cars around. A little before rush hour, say, six-thirty or so . . . yeah, no problem, we'll talk."

Matthews hung up.

The girl stood up and approached Matthews, her eyes shining, the color high in her cheeks, and ignoring Weinstein totally.

"You're going to kill him, aren't you?"

Matthews looked at her, saying nothing.

"You are," she said, reaching slowly up and touching his lips with her fingertips. "I can tell, now."

"Are you going to be a good girl?" Matthews asked. "Or do I have to tie you up, too?"

Wordlessly the girl stepped back, still staring into Matthews's eyes, and unclipped the straps of her overalls, dropping them to the floor.

She wore no underwear. She had shaved her pubis, whether motivated by art or crabs Matthews could not guess, and standing before him, her pants around her ankles, her body looked like a child's.

"Would you *like* to tie me up?" she asked.

When Matthews did not respond, she turned and knelt on the bed, offering him her buttocks. With her knees apart and her weight on her elbows, she no longer looked like a child at all.

"You can hurt me, too, if you want," she said, turning her head and smiling over her shoulder at Matthews, "as long as it's *fun* hurt."

Matthews said nothing for a moment, then sighed and nodded. At his direction, she placed her hands behind her back, where he bound them with another strip of sheet. Then, standing beside her as she watched, eyes shining, he slowly undid his belt buckle and withdrew the belt from his pants. When she saw what he was doing she gave a small gasp, then turned and buried her face in the mattress, her buttocks up-turned and expectant.

Bending, Matthews passed the belt around her ankles and snugged them tight, then dragged her like a laundry bag across the living room floor into the bathroom. There he lifted her into the tub and tied the loose end of the belt to the handle of the cold water faucet. Bidding her good night and cautioning her against excessive motion, he slid the shower curtain to, extinguished the light, and closed the door.

It was six-fifteen by Matthews's watch when a dull sepia glow in the window facing the airshaft began to announce the dawn. The naked girl was trembling with cold when he entered the bathroom, and Matthews carefully set the water to warm before starting the shower to muffle any noise. Returning to the living room, Matthews filled a glass with Cognac, then unbound and ungagged Weinstein, pulling him to his feet where he tottered unsteadily.

"Drink it," Matthews said, handing him the glass.

"You gotta listen to me," Weinstein said, controlling his voice with enormous effort. "It's not what you . . ."

"Drink it," Matthews repeated.

Weinstein had half finished the Cognac, gagging, when Matthews struck him again in the stomach, this time catching him before he could hit the floor. Together they descended the stairs, Matthews easily supporting Weinstein's weight. The only comment they elicited came from the owner of the bodega, whom they passed in the hallway, who, wrinkling his nose at the stench of brandy and vomitus that glistened on Weinstein's chin, observed with some asperity that if a man could not hold his liquor he should not be permitted to drink it.

The car was a metallic blue Plymouth Fury, four door, with no inside handles on the rear doors. The two men who rode in the front seat might have come directly from an open casting call for *The Godfather*. The driver wore a black leather jacket and mirrored sunglasses. His long black hair was lovingly combed back and reeked of cologne. The man in the passenger seat, broad of shoulder, low of brow, and with narrow-set pig eyes, looked like Koko the Gorilla in a pilled corduroy car coat.

"Ya get any of that puke onna car seat," Koko growled, reaching back and stabbing Weinstein in the chest with a thick forefinger, "an' we'll hafta kill ya."

The driver cackled.

Weinstein swallowed and turned to Matthews, who rode looking straight ahead.

"Please," he said, "please. You gotta listen to me."

"Sure," Matthews said indifferently, "go ahead."

"I didn't set you up," Weinstein said in a voice as even as he could make it. "The cops were there for me, not you."

"Uh-huh," said Matthews.

"Listen," Weinstein continued, his voice becoming more urgent, "you've read about the Fifteenth of June Group, right?"

"Nope," said Matthews.

"Sure you have," pleaded Weinstein, "there was a bomb, out in Connecticut, a guy got killed, some scientist. It's been front page for the last week." Weinstein was sufficiently desperate to appeal to the man in the front seat. "How about you? You've read about it, right?" But Koko was busy devouring a cuticle and had nothing for Weinstein but a low growl.

"For Christ's sake," he moaned, "doesn't anybody read the fucking papers? The Fifteenth of June Group, that's me! Me and Priscilla!"

"Let me see if I've got it straight," Matthews finally said. "You and the blond featherhead that we just left are wanted by the FBI for blowing up scientists, and it was just some sort of coincidence that the ATF boys had your building staked out when I showed up to sell you a gun. Is that it?"

"Yes!" Weinstein babbled excitedly, "that's . . ."

"You little asshole," Matthews said. "You couldn't blow up a balloon."

"Right!" Weinstein agreed frantically. "That's the thing! It wasn't us, see, it was this German guy, calls himself Andreas, that I met a few weeks ago in Washington Square Park. He used our name! He and Priscilla got tight, and he used this chick named Fran who was hanging around Priscilla to plant the bomb, and then he killed her, too! That's why the cops were . . ."

Matthews sighed, his face troubled. "I don't want to see you get hurt for the wrong reason, my friend," he said, "but without names, or addresses, or stuff I could maybe check, I'm having a hard time believing you. Maybe you should try a little harder."

For the next half-hour, as the four of them drove around lower Manhattan, Weinstein tried very hard indeed, clutching at Matthews's infrequent questions as a drowning man would a thrown line. When at last he was empty, spent and weeping, Matthews tapped the driver on the shoulder.

"Drop me on West Thirteenth Street," he said.

The car stopped on Thirteenth Street west of Fifth Avenue. The gorilla opened the door for Matthews and slid in next to Weinstein as Matthews got out.

"Please," wept Weinstein, "please, you gotta believe me."

"I do," Matthews said.

"What?" whispered Weinstein, watching with the eyes of a rabbit sharing a back seat with a boa constrictor as Koko reached slowly into the pocket of his car coat. When he removed his thick hand and opened it, he was holding a badge in a leather case.

"FBI, motherfucker," Koko said, pulling the door closed, "and I was serious about getting any of that goddamned stuff on the seats."

Matthews stood in front of the Quad Cinema, watching, as the car pulled into traffic and disappeared. Then, oblivious to the censorious stares of the early morning commuters on their way to the F train, he bent to the gutter, his hands on his knees, and vomited violently, again and again.

CHAPTER THIRTEEN

THE call from the Federal Correctional Facility at Allenwood had been patched through to Stuarti at 6:45 the previous evening, and even the greenest trainee would surely have remarked that, for a man of his experience, he handled it very poorly indeed.

Identifying himself as a "Hudson from Legal"—so unconvincingly that he was mockingly addressed as such for the remainder of the conversation—Stuarti apologized for the hour and explained, somewhat stumblingly, the purpose of his call. It had come to Legal's attention, Stuarti said, that his interlocutor was considering a motion for retrial on the grounds that his original plea had been coerced. Such coercion, Stuarti explained, was as contrary to Agency policy as it was to federal law, and if on review a directed dismissal should turn out to be the cost of putting the Agency's legal house in order, well, probity had no price.

How had this come to "Legal's" attention? Well, rumor really, Stuarti explained awkwardly. No, no papers had actually been filed, but it was said that—Continue the discussion by letter? With copies to the lawyers concerned? Oh, no need, laughed Stuarti, in a dreadfully failed attempt at ingratiation; it was to obviate, if possible, the tedium of needless paperwork that he had called. . . . By which time Stuarti was in such disordered retreat that the mere suggestion that his superiors be involved obliged him helplessly to confess that *actually*, he was calling less in his strictly official capacity than as a favor to a friend—a *mutual* friend, he added portentously—to whose concerned attention the retrial rumors had come.

Here the tone of the conversation changed abruptly, the mocking bitterness of Stuarti's interlocutor evaporating and fear, naked and undisguisable, taking its place.

"Listen to me, Hudson-from-Legal, and listen good," the man hissed, the breath whistling in his teeth. "Our friend said he wanted a plea and the names, and he *got* the goddamned plea and the names! That was the deal then, and it's still the deal. You tell him that. No motions, no retrial, no noise at all. Make goddamned sure that he understands that anything else he hears is bullshit!"

"Actually," Stuarti replied hesitantly, "there seems to be some question about the names . . ."

"Forget it," the man said firmly, his voice suddenly alert, but Stuarti, having elicited the mention of "the names," was by then no longer Hudson-from-Legal, but rather an anonymous and ice-cold voice on the phone, who in the five minutes that followed convincingly demonstrated that a weak man in prison belongs to whoever leans on him hardest, longest, and last.

When Minihan arrived at the Thirteenth Street townhouse shortly before seven in the morning, it was clear that Stuarti had not slept.

Cheeks stubbled, sparse gray hair standing out wildly from his head, and robed in his mandarin dressing gown, Stuarti was parked before the window, code-name Bunny's personal file spread out on a card table before him. The papers were neatly stacked and arranged and labeled topically: Family

History, Education, Travel, Employment History, Friends and Associates, Papers and Periodicals ... there were perhaps twenty piles. When Minihan entered, Stuarti was working through the stack marked Travel, winnowing recent credit card slips from the pile and occasionally scribbling on his clipboard.

"Your man Matthews is out safely," Minihan said as he entered. "My people picked them up on East Sixth Street fifteen minutes ago. I just got it on the car phone."

Stuarti exhaled long and slowly, slumping in the wheelchair and putting his clipboard, facedown, on the table.

"Good," he said, sighing again and pressing the heels of his hands against his eyes. "I may be getting a little old for these all-nighters. What've you got there?"

"Surveillance reports on our customer for the past forty-eight hours," Minihan said, swinging his briefcase onto the couch. "Also summary logs of the taps, with concordance transcripts ..."

"With *what*?"

"Transcripts without the uh's and the duh's and the fluh's," Minihan said. "Just the stuff you can understand."

"What about the other hand, Frank?"

"This?" Minihan said, holding up a brown paper bag.

"Don't screw around, Frank," Stuarti said sternly. "You're talking to a starving man. I sent Floyd out last night, told him to get us some emergency food for the duration, and the silly bastard came back with a dozen cans of corned-beef hash and a case of evaporated milk. It must have been the word emergency. Tell me it's pastry, Frank."

"It's pastry," Minihan said.

"Bless you," Stuarti said, taking the bag and arranging a paper napkin on his lap. "Now what about the other stuff?"

"Interesting, actually," Minihan said, seating himself on the couch. "It's way too early to be sure, of course, but we've got a conversation between him and some woman named

97

Berg, which you might want to read twice, because I think we're going to have to take a look at her. It's the yellow flag in the transcript, there. . . . What's the matter?"

Stuarti's face was tragic.

"Somebody ran over my jelly doughnut, Frank."

"It's not a jelly doughnut," Minihan sighed. "It's a prune Danish."

"A *what*?"

"Matthews," announced Stuarti's Mormon from the door, as if there were not very much that he could do about it.

"Let me ask you this," Stuarti snapped without preamble as Matthews entered, regarding with uncompromising hostility the newly unwrapped pastry on the table before him. "Have you ever, in your life, heard of something called a *prune Danish*?"

"Sure," Matthews said. His face was pale and he smelled faintly of Scope.

"Bullshit," Stuarti grumbled. "Not even the *Danes* have ever heard of a prune Danish. It's a sad goddamned business, having to watch old friends get so senile that they can't even tell the difference between a jelly doughnut and some godawful laxative bun. Speaking of which, this's Frank Minihan, our Bureau liaison to the IG."

Matthews and Minihan shook hands, gravely.

"Frank's family," Stuarti said, "despite the pastry trick. What'd Weinstein have to say?"

"Everything he could think of," Matthews said, sitting and helping himself to a sip of Stuarti's coffee, "which actually wasn't all that much that we didn't already know or hadn't already guessed. There's a mean new friend, all right, but it turns out to be Priscilla No-Last-Name's friend, not Weinstein's, and she would've fed poor Markie to the fish rather than talk about him. Weinstein wasn't real pleased to find out he'd been traded in, and gave me everything he had, but it wasn't much."

"Go ahead," Stuarti said sulkily, tearing off a piece of pastry uncontaminated by prune paste and popping it into his mouth.

"Early thirties, blond hair, chunky, maybe five-ten," Matthews said. "Uses the first name Andreas, no last name, and Weinstein also made him as a German, so the accent must be obvious. The guy picked Weinstein up in Washington Square Park about four weeks ago, and met Priscilla through him. Some time after that, Weinstein thinks, the guy showed Priscilla something that impressed the hell out of her, but he doesn't know what it is, and she won't tell, save to say loftily that 'Andreas takes his politics seriously' . . ."

"Two murders in the last two weeks," Stuarti observed, swallowing. "That's being serious almost to the point of humorlessness."

"Apparently *he* contacts *her*," Matthews continued. "At least Weinstein's never heard her mention an address."

"Let me get this straight," Stuarti said, patting his lips delicately with a paper napkin. "No last name for our friend Andreas, no address, and no idea where he is. Am I going to have to tell Harold that he jeopardized his marriage and threw up on himself for nothing?"

"I don't think so," Matthews said. "Weinstein and Priscilla No-Last-Name are not only the only two people who can *identify* Andreas, they're also, given the fact that they constitute the entire Fifteenth of June Group, the only two people who could plausibly put the proposition that there ever *was* an Andreas. For him, they represent dangerous loose ends that need tying up. The girl knows my notional first name, where I work, and the fact that I've recently been paroled from Green Haven, all of which will check out if they bother, and they will. Sooner or later, Andreas is going to have to know what happened to Weinstein, and when he does, he'll send the girl."

"Or come himself," Stuarti observed.

"If we're lucky," Matthews responded, in a voice chillingly

99

devoid of affect. Standing, Matthews drained Stuarti's coffee and returned the cup to the table.

"I have to go to work," he said. "I'm on at the gym today from eight 'til two."

"Anything you need?" Stuarti asked.

"Yes," Matthews said. "Have the Bureau boys and a city SWAT team toss Weinstein's apartment. Tell them to stand on the sidewalk and yell through a bullhorn a few times before they kick the door down, in case any of the neighbors are asleep and might miss it otherwise."

"Anything else?" Stuarti asked, scribbling on his clipboard. "Money, that sort of thing?"

"I shouldn't think so," Matthews said, baring his teeth in what he intended as a smile. "My new job pays me four dollars an hour to encourage fat guys to do sit-ups, and if I need more than that I can always take it from one of them."

Minihan's head rose slowly, looking first at Matthews, then at Stuarti.

"Of course," Stuarti said brightly, to his credit managing a smile. "And you'll be in touch?"

"Yes," Matthews said from the door, without turning.

"Mind how you go, dear boy," Stuarti said.

"Your ferret seems a little edgy," Minihan finally observed.

"Perhaps he had a restless night," Stuarti replied shortly.

"I understand he whomped Weinstein around pretty good," Minihan said. "They told me the guy couldn't even *walk* when Matthews brought him out."

"Tough," Stuarti said. "Run around playing games with guns and bombs, there's always a chance you might run into an actual hard guy somewhere along the line."

"It's not that," Minihan said. "But if our friend Bunny ever comes to trial it's likely that the prosecution'd want to call Weinstein. And while the Supreme Court doesn't seem to mind these days, what with Rehnquist and all, the United

States Court for the Southern District of New York still frowns on whaling the piss out of witnesses."

"You've got to stop talking about trials and witnesses, Frank," Stuarti said fretfully. "When we talk about code-name Bunny we're talking about a young man on the way up, not some kind of crook."

"I beg your pardon?" Minihan said.

"Yup," Stuarti said proudly. "Our boy's coming up in the world. In fact, he was named Friday to replace Butterfield as the ACDA's technical support representative to the Sackpig."

"To the *what*?"

"SACPG," Stuarti said. "The Senior Arms Control Policy Group. They pronounce it Sackpig. The Joint Chiefs, plus senior representatives from the NSC, Defense, and State. The ACDA sends a representative to stand around, in case the big boys need some charts or numbers that they might not have. It used to be Butterfield's job. Who better than his trusted deputy, we asked ourselves, to fill his fallen leader's shoes?"

"Are you out of your mind?" Minihan demanded.

"What do you mean?" Stuarti said. "Wouldn't you want cabinet-level access if *you* were a Soviet spy?"

"The director's going to puke," Minihan said glumly.

"Actually," Stuarti continued brightly, "it occurred to me that the director might not be too comfy with the idea, and after all, why should *he* take a risk? Tell him that we'll take full responsibility for monitoring and restricting Bunny's access from here on out. Hell, we'll even put it in writing if he wants."

"Ed?"

"Yes, Frank?"

"You wouldn't try to blow a high hard one past an old friend, would you?"

"Certainly not, Frank," Stuarti said, his tone hurt. " 'Course the director's a different story." Stuarti picked up an envelope from the table. "I had the lawyers in our shop draft this. His initials'll do just fine."

"You want Bureau permission to control the subject's access," Minihan said, gingerly taking the envelope, "and you want it in writing, *bad*, is the way I get it."

"An intriguing interpretation, Frank," Stuarti said. "Perhaps you'd be so good as to keep it to yourself. Listen, I need a favor."

"Nothing but, far's I can tell," Minihan said sourly.

Reaching to the couch and delving into the pocket of his cape—which he had worn around his shoulders in the night, for warmth—Stuarti exhumed first several used Kleenexes from the previous winter, then two cinema stubs from the Gaumont-Élysées, and finally a scrap of lined notebook paper that he unfolded, read, and handed to Minihan.

"I'd like you to check out a couple of names for me," Stuarti said. "The guys are both IRA leg-breakers, live in the Inwood section of Manhattan, and hang out at the Donemay Pub. Whoever you've got in NORAID this month should be able to help us out."

"Any special reason you don't want to feed this one through Langley?" Minihan asked.

"I suppose I could," Stuarti sighed, "but then what'd be the point of having a friend in the FBI?"

"What do you want to know about them?" Minihan asked.

"I'd just like to keep tabs on their health," Stuarti said brightly. "Either of 'em catch a cold or anything, I'd like to know."

"Ed . . ." Minihan began, but Stuarti, glancing suddenly at his watch, had no more time to give the subject.

"Christ, Frank, it's five past!" he said, wheeling his chair around and scooting toward the television. "We're going to miss 'Mr. Rogers'!"

"Miss what?" Minihan asked carefully.

"It's this terrific TV show," Stuarti said eagerly. "This guy sits right up at the front of the tube, looks you square in the eye, and then starts talkin' about two miles an hour about stuff like feeding the fish and visiting the postman. I figure he's on reds, but who cares? Listening to the guy for fifteen minutes is better than a fistful of Librium. Trust me, Frank, it's a hell of a show. I think you'd . . ."

"Stop it!" Minihan ordered, standing abruptly. "I'm having a hard enough time reassuring the director as it is!"

"Yesterday there were hamsters," Stuarti said enticingly.

"I'll be back tomorrow morning," Minihan said firmly, and as he closed the door behind him, leaving Stuarti, face rapt, before the television, he could hear a soothing voice singing gently, "Will you be? Won't you be? Please will you be . . . my neighbor!"

CHAPTER FOURTEEN

MATTHEWS'S shift at the gym ended the following Wednesday, without call or visitor, at two in the afternoon, and it was not until he had showered and changed that he realized that he would that day go to Kate.

From Twelfth Street Matthews took the local subway to Thirty-fourth, where, after twenty minutes spent cleaning his back in Macy's, he retrieved his car from a nearby parking garage. By 2:45 he was heading north in light traffic on the West Side Highway, the radio tuned to an Italian station broadcasting from Paterson, New Jersey on which, with Calabrian vehemence, an announcer was excoriating the manifold sins of George Steinbrenner.

The languages had been a gift from his father; indeed, along with an inexplicably battered briefcase from Mark Cross, had been his sole patrimony. The son of a shipping magnate, Matthews's father had been raised, poorly, on three continents, and though he himself had mastered no tongue but his own believed firmly, and asserted often, that to acquire a foreign language was to possess another soul. The precise utility of multiple souls—or of Italian, for that matter—was never entirely clear to Matthews as a boy, save, as best he understood it, as a general specific against the fate of the Many Too Many; against a life of restriction and convention, pervasive boredom, stifling domestic limits, and social falsity. Indeed, hearing happiness called names had been a childhood commonplace, for Matthews's father believed an overconcern for matters merely utilitarian to be irredeemably vulgar; a belief that, though it had lent elegance to his manners, had served him less well when, in his fiftieth year and Matthews's eighth, the family money had changed owners, leaving him as dislocated in time and place, and as stumped for a strategy, as a Galapagos tortoise in Grand Central. Matthews's boyishly meagre resources—no matter how frantically deployed—had proved insufficient to tempt him lifeward, and within twelve months he had died; of embarrassment, disappointment, and an irrelevant and face-saving carcinoma of the lung.

As he passed a construction zone beneath the George Washington Bridge, his eyes stinging with sleeplessness, Matthews wondered briefly if his father, too, as he slid toward death, had found himself daydreaming of complete conformity, as another person, from a different life, might have dreamed of winning Wimbledon or the Irish Sweeps.

The sky above was the purest blue, the shattering clatter of the road crew's jackhammers swelled and receded in an air so clear it seemed of a liquid density, and above the Hudson, swollen by spring flood and freighted with eggshell and orange peel, white gulls floated silently as seraphim on the thermals, wings unmoving, raw red hands dangling limply beneath them, as though, perhaps, they had been crushed.

Stuarti, on the Washington line to Irving the Office Manager, was irritable and short. He was deeply tired, the apartment was hot, and his Mormon, sporting a new glen plaid suit (and a plain gray machine pistol), had for the past half-hour been pacing constantly between the two curtained windows of the living room with the jerky homicidal alertness of a young Doberman, passing, each time he did so, between Stuarti and "General Hospital."

"Of *course* I care about the provenance of the xerography paper, Irving," Stuarti said testily, "I just don't give a shit if it's Czech or East German . . . That's right . . ." Stuarti sighed noisily, listened. "Then *get* a Siemens impact printer. Also put in a mock bank of secure phones, clearly marked as to service. . . . Christ, Irving, we've already been over this a thousand times! Whatever your technical people decide about the film and the processing marks is fine with me. . . . No, Irving, I'm not mad at you, and thank you, yes, I realize the importance of the details. In fact, it was your unerring instinct for the capillary that got you this assignment. . . . No, no, Irving, just a little joke, my way of relieving the tension . . . yes, Irving, I suppose I could. In fact, now that you mention it, another way *does* come to mind."

With a thunderous crash, Stuarti slammed the telephone receiver into the cradle, in the process scaring the shit out of his Mormon and coming within an eyelash of being machine-gunned to death.

Continuing north, first on the Sawmill River Parkway and then on Route 684, Matthews passed through wealthy suburbs, horse country. After the cold dark months of crystalline suspension leaves were everywhere unfolding, the trees like green beings not yet wholly awake, still held in an iridescent chrysalis of tentative color and vibrant air.

In Brewster the traffic was slowed to a crawl by an accident. A car exiting from Heidi's Motel onto Route 22 had been rammed from the rear by another, and though the injured had already been transported, the area was still swarming with volunteer firemen and EMTs in Dyna-Med jackets with reflective sleeves, all stern and radiant with the emotion of dashing forth at breakneck speed to do good.

Had this, then, been what had followed in his wake, Matthews wondered. The broken glass, the stunned witnesses, discarded compresses stained with blood littering the verge?

If so, Matthews thought savagely, teeth locked and nostrils flaring, there had been a hell of a lot of trouble for nothing, for in an advanced society, as Durkheim had taught, the division of labor replaces the *conscience commune*, and what Matthews (himself a specialist) had taken apart, not all the king's horses nor all the king's men . . .

Abruptly turning on his signal light, Matthews pulled into the parking lot of the Red Rooster Drive-In and waited there, quite patiently, for the now familiar trembling to stop.

"General Hospital" over, and his chastened Mormon dispatched for pizza, Stuarti was again on the Washington line, this time harassing, and being harassed by, Eliot the Casting Director.

"Let me tell you *again*, then, Eliot," he said, "and this time pay attention, take notes, whatever it is you have to do . . . I *know* it's difficult, and yes, I'm sympathetic. It can't be easy having Alzheimer's at your age. Got a pencil? All right. Now we've got the *real* secretary of defense for a maximum of seven minutes, less depending on the travel time, and since we can't trust the bastard to *remember* any lines, we're not going to *give* him any lines. All he has to do is open the meeting, thank the Group for their work, remind them of the responsibility involved in drafting a National Security Decision Directive, and say that he'll be available in the adjacent conference room if they need him. Then he exits left into the small conference room, and with any luck is back across the river with his luncheon meeting inside a total elapsed time of twenty minutes. That's where *your* secretary of defense comes in. We'll leave the door to the small conference room open occasionally, and all he has to do, really, is to walk by it two or three times. Your Joint Chiefs are going to be going in to consult during the afternoon and coming out and saying stuff

107

like, 'The secretary wonders about this,' and 'The secretary'd like to see that,' so really all Bunny needs to do is see the guy's back a few times. . . . C'mon, Eliot, how tough can it be to find a truculent dwarf with a jet black rug? It can even *look* like a rug. . . . That's right, no speaking part at all. . . . No, I'll be down tonight or tomorrow morning on the shuttle. Tell Bullard to pick me up at the L'Enfant Plaza at noon. And Eliot, tell Irving that he's got to learn to keep his voice down if he's going to stand next to the phone. Not all 'old farts' are deaf."

Checking carefully first to be certain that his Mormon had not returned unnoticed, Stuarti again, with rich satisfaction, slammed the phone into the cradle.

Matthews left Route 22 at Wingdale, N.Y., crossing the border into Connecticut and heading north on Route 7 into the small town of Kent. It was only as he entered the village that he dimly realized that he had not called Kate, and that it was thus possible that she did not know that he was coming.

Matthews called the cottage from the pay phone outside the Fife and Drum restaurant. The phone rang six times without response. Waiting, it never occurred to Matthews that she would not answer.

On the seventh ring she did.

"Hello, Kate?" Matthews said softly, unable to recognize his own voice as he spoke. "It's me."

"Oh, Tom!" she gasped, the sudden catch in her breath sweetly familiar in his ear. "Oh, thank God, I was in the shower and I almost let it ring! Where are you?"

"I'm in the village . . ." Matthews said.

"It must be Kismet," Kate said happily. "You'll never guess what I just washed."

"Shall I pick anything up?" Matthews asked.

"Oh, no," Kate said. "Please hurry."

* * *

The road that led up Skiff Mountain from the river valley to the cottage was vividly shadowed, canopied in new green. The car filled with the scent of woodland air, and the clarity and variety of evening birdsong would have seemed startling in its racket had Matthews not been nearly deafened by the blood roar in his ears.

And then, upon him as suddenly as an apparition, there was the driveway, a narrow dirt road rutted by winter along which he jolted between tangled banks of flowering lilac, to emerge into the clearing where the cottage stood, the distant valley yawning away behind it and Kate, not distant at all, standing on its raised porch.

She wore sandals and a sundress of a blue that would have seemed vivid had it not been for her eyes. Her black hair was still wet from the shower, her limbs were strong and tan and lovely, and her face, save for high spots of color on her cheekbones, was burning white.

Matthews emerged from the car and stood by it, holding her as steadily in his gaze as he had for the past week held her in the basin of his mind. Together they regarded one another, unmoving.

"What a lovely surprise," Kate said gently.

"For me, too," Matthews said. "I didn't know that I was coming, or I'd have called ahead."

"Are you through?" Kate asked. "Or was this just a slow day in the game of nations?"

"I have to be back tomorrow morning," Matthews said.

Kate accepted this with equanimity, her face nowhere showing the stab of disappointment that she felt, within.

"I've made an intriguing discovery in your absence," Kate said. "Would you like to hear about it?"

"Yes," Matthews said.

"Do you remember the night that you came to the hospital and carried me away on your roan rent-a-car?" Kate smiled.

109

"That was months ago," Matthews smiled back. "A person can't remember everything."

"You told me then," Kate continued, ignoring him, "when you gave me the papers that would make me Miss Farrington, that you had found an inexpensive rental in Litchfield County. Two hundred a month, heat included, the checks payable to Casey Realty as agent for the owner. Ring a bell?"

"Vaguely," Matthews said.

"Good," Kate said. "Well, it occurred to me this week that I might want to explore the possibility of extending my lease. When Casey gave me the runaround, informing me rather archly that he wasn't at liberty to reveal the owner's name, I decided that if I wanted any real information I'd better go to the source. So I buttonholed Mrs. Mulready."

"And?" Matthews said.

"She's a dear woman, Tom," Kate said, "but a terrible liar. Unless, of course, she wanted me to know."

"Know what?"

"That I've been sleeping with my landlord," Kate said.

"Would you have come if you'd known?" Matthews asked gravely. "Would you have stayed?"

"I don't know," Kate said. "Though I know now I'd like to stay."

"What else did you learn while I was gone?" Matthews asked, softly taking her hands in his.

"Lots," Kate said brightly, loving him with her eyes. "I'm a city girl, and there's tons to learn. Did you know, for instance, that an American tree sparrow has twice as many vertebrae in its neck as a giraffe?"

"No," Matthews said, kissing her hand and pressing it softly against his cheek.

"It's true," she said, her voice thickening slightly. "And the spores of a puffball mushroom are so light that they're taken up into the atmosphere and descend to earth as the nuclei of raindrops . . ."

Her breath came more rapidly and a tiny tremor passed

through her legs as Matthews turned her other hand over and lingeringly kissed her open palm.

"What else?" Matthews asked, his lips and breath against her skin raising goosebumps as he spoke.

"Well," she sighed, "a raccoon has this bone in its penis, called a baculum . . ."

Here Matthews, standing two steps beneath her, wrapped his arms gently around her hips and drew her to him, his face pressing against her belly, and when Kate, naked beneath the sundress, lifted her skirt in order to pull him more closely to her, the gesture seemed less that of a wanton lover than that of a thoughtful hostess, generously sharing the only woman's body that they had.

Waiting for Minihan's call while his Mormon did calisthenics in the kitchen, Stuarti sat slumped in the wheelchair peering sullenly into his new aquarium. On the pastel pebbles that lined the bottom a tiny deep-sea diver lay on his side, a stream of bubbles issuing from his helmet; drowning, Stuarti assumed, and understandably undiverted by the plastic mermaid leering nearby. Pressed against the glass wall a miniature grouper was practicing smoke rings, as it had incessantly since its arrival that afternoon, while behind it, partially hidden by a clump of kelp, a tattered silver angelfish was being nibbled to death by neons.

When the phone sounded, Stuarti answered it before it had finished ringing for the first time.

"I've got the information on your NORAID guys," Minihan said, his voice oddly sober. "The thugs whose health you wanted to keep tabs on."

"And?" Stuarti said.

"Not healthy at *all*," Minihan said. "One's in his fourth month in the ICU up at Lincoln Hospital. The other's made it as far as Rehab, but it seems he's still got some recurring problem with his spleen."

"I see," Stuarti said carefully. "Car accident?"

"No," Minihan said. "One of them caught it outside his job on One Hundred Thirty-third Street. The A and L Meat Company. Some guys just came out of nowhere, jerked him into the garage bay, and left him with more broken bones than Evel Knievel. They found the other guy about the same time, tossed behind some bushes in Isham Park. The ER report I saw would seem to suggest that he might've had the same visitor."

"When did this happen, Frank?"

"December twenty-sixth," said Minihan after a moment. "The bench guy got called in at twelve-forty, the meat company guy at one-oh-five that afternoon."

"Maybe it's how the Irish do Boxing Day," Stuarti said. "Who's handling it?"

"Midtown North," Minihan said. "But they weren't too fond of the guys anyway, and they've got a lot on their plates."

"Witnesses?" Stuarti asked.

"For the meat company guy only, I think," Minihan said. "I can ask."

"Maybe you could just look at the file instead of asking, Frank," Stuarti said. "And I'd like the names and addresses."

"You're making me a little uneasy, Ed," Minihan said.

"Take drugs for it," Stuarti said. "That's what everybody else does. Although as a friend I'd advise you to try 'Mr. Rogers' first. See you tomorrow morning, usual time?"

"Yes," Minihan said.

Hanging up without further conversation, Stuarti breathed deeply once, then extended his arms, fingers waggling, and addressed his Mormon.

"Help me out of this thing," he said, "and then help me get a cab. I'm going down to Washington on the shuttle tonight. I'll be back the day after tomorrow."

"Do you want me to drive you to the airport?" the young man asked.

"*No,*" Stuarti said sternly, shuddering at the thought of

his armed Mormon in traffic on the Brooklyn-Queens Expressway. "Just hand me some socks and undies from the other bag."

"Do you want me to feed the fish?" the Mormon asked.

"Fuck the fish," said Stuarti.

CHAPTER FIFTEEN

WHEN Bullard arrived at noon to pick him up, Stuarti, wearing his traveling cape and beret and drinking a split of champagne, was already parked, waiting, in the lobby of Washington's L'Enfant Plaza Hotel.

"What in God's name," Bullard gritted as he wheeled Stuarti rapidly through the lobby to a car waiting at the curb outside, "is the meaning of that outlandish getup?"

"What do you mean?" Stuarti asked in a puzzled tone, looking down. "This is my formal outfit, the one I always wear for visits to the nation's capital."

"I see," said Bullard, grim-faced, as he put on the parking brake and began to help Stuarti from the wheelchair.

"Hey, listen, Bullard," Stuarti said brightly, "Thanks a lot for the fish. I was touched. No one's ever given me a live fish before. Or even considered it, far's I know."

"Well," Bullard said, his features relenting slightly as he lowered Stuarti onto the front seat of the car, "I felt a teensy bit guilty about snapping at you the other day, and thought perhaps you might enjoy some company in that dreadful little apartment. Be careful not to overfeed the silver angel."

"I don't think you need to worry about that," Stuarti said reassuringly as they traversed the Mall and turned left on Constitution Avenue.

"Why not?" Bullard demanded suspiciously. "What have you been giving them?"

"Leftovers, mostly," Stuarti said absently. "Did you know that pizza floats?"

It was in silence, therefore, that they passed the Ellipse, turned right on Eighteenth Street for four blocks, then right again on F Street. Before them loomed the rear of the Old Executive Office Building, which was their destination, around which Stuarti could see a portion of the White House lawn.

"Is this the way Bunny will come in?" Stuarti asked, as they had their identification checked at the rear entrance to the EOB.

"We'll take him in through the front," Bullard replied coldly, "and let him have a nice long look at the White House. Other than that the route's the same."

"And how about our people?" Stuarti asked, as Bullard began to wheel him down the corridor.

"Eight through the front door over a period of twenty minutes," Bullard said, "and the other six through here. They'll be using their own IDs, same as today, and wearing civvies. Eliot's already got the uniforms upstairs."

"Is Dr. Doom here?" Stuarti asked.

"Professor Quade is waiting upstairs with the others," Bullard said. "And *please* don't call him Dr. Doom."

Together Bullard and Stuarti took an elevator from the front entrance bank to the third floor of the EOB. Turning right, they continued down the corridor for perhaps fifty yards, pausing finally before an imposing set of mahogany double doors. While a heavy bronze plaque identified the office complex behind the doors as that of the Southwest Asian Working Group, a paper sign crudely lettered in pencil CLOSED FOR ALTERATIONS and a welter of paint cans, sawhorses, and spattered tarpaulins indicated that the problems of Southwest Asia were, at least temporarily, being resolved elsewhere.

"The plaque's magnetic," Bullard explained, knocking. "Takes about two seconds to change. We'll shift the rest of the stuff one door down when he hits the building, and then back in front again once he's inside."

The door was opened a crack by a silver-haired, scowling painter dressed in spattered coveralls and holding a wet roller. Seeing Bullard, he opened the door sufficiently for them to enter and then closed it behind them, fast. Inside, the anteroom was spotlessly neat.

"This's Hobbes," Bullard said. "He's from Archives, and he's going to be our chief of naval operations."

"It's an honor, Mr. Stuarti, sir," the silver-haired man said, wiping his hand on his coveralls and nearly curtsying with deference as he gingerly replaced the roller in its pan on a newspaper. "You're one of our very *favorites* in Archives."

"Same here," Stuarti said, shaking the one finger that he could find without paint on it. "I've always had a weakness for sailors, myself."

"The complex has four rooms," Bullard interrupted hurriedly. "The large conference room, the small conference room giving off it with access back to what we're calling Office B, over there, and this anteroom. We'll use Office B for a command post and changing room. We'll have two Marines in dress uniform here in the anteroom, nominally for security, but also to act as a buffer should we need one . . ."

"Dress uniform?" Stuarti asked.

"It's Eliot," Bullard sighed. "He says the dress uniform has more éclat, and refuses to budge."

"Why not?" Stuarti shrugged.

They entered the large conference room to a babble of voices. On one side of a long felt-topped conference table that dominated the room perhaps a dozen men sat and stood, chatting easily. On the other side of the table an elderly man whom Stuarti took to be Professor Quade sat in clenched distaste, listening with rigid features to Harold-Who-Does-the-Disgusting-Things's animated discussion of the relative tensile strength of colostomy bags.

On seeing Stuarti and Bullard, an emaciated figure with wavy pink hair and half-glasses leaped to his feet and hurried to them, his gait that of a stork in a footrace to the death.

"Edward," he murmured lovingly, tucking a clipboard under his arm and extending both hands. *"Ça fait trop long-temps . . ."*

"Longtemps, anyway," Stuarti said shortly. "Listen, Eliot, you might want to think twice about dressing up those Marines. The last person to try that was Nixon, and you know what happened to *him.*"

"I know," Eliot sighed dreamily. "He's a millionaire and lives in Saddle River. *Places, everyone!"*

As everyone moved to their assigned chairs, the noise in the room slowly abated until the only voice to be heard was Harold's.

"Trust me," he was saying earnestly to Professor Quade, who clearly did not, "when you're talking state of the art, you're talking Mylar bag . . ."

"For Christ's sake, Harold," Stuarti said impatiently. "Snap out of it. Who're you supposed to be?"

"Under secretary of defense for policy," Harold replied, sulking.

"Then go to your goddamned chair," Stuarti said.

"This *is* my chair," Harold said.

Stuarti, detecting archness in the tone, glanced sharply at Harold for a moment, then turned to Eliot the Casting Director.

"OK, Eliot," he said. "Gimme the rundown by chair."

"Exclusive of backstage personnel," Eliot began, no longer dreamy at all, "we have a total cast of fourteen, fifteen if we count the secretary of defense's cameo. The seating will be

117

by rank and service from the head of the table, as follows." Pointing to each of the men in turn, Eliot began to identify the cast by role. "Deputy national security adviser," he said, "who will chair. From the Joint Chiefs, we have the chairman, JCS, and the chief of Naval Operations, plus a senior representative from each of the other two services. The detailed DOD position will be argued by the under secretary of defense for policy who, as you just heard, will be played by Harold. From State, we've got the director, State Department Bureau of Politico-Military Affairs—Michaels is actually a pretty good look-alike—plus two P.A.s. And, of course, Professor Quade and the technical support representative—our customer— from the ACDA. Two male stenographers inside and the two Marines outside bring it to fifteen, but none of them have speaking parts and I decided we didn't need to risk bringing them in today."

"What about your deputy national security adviser?" Stuarti demanded. "The guy was only appointed two months ago, and he probably had his face in the papers or on the tube. Bunny might have . . ."

Eliot picked up his clipboard, turned several pages, and read aloud. "*Washington Post*, sixteen March, second section inside. Our customer doesn't get the *Washington Post*. *The New York Times*, seventeen March, page eight, a photo that must be the guy's high school graduation picture. No problem there. 'CBS Evening News,' ten days ago, a four-second shot in the context of another story. According to the surveillance reports, our customer was on the Lexington Avenue IRT during the news. If you want a better look-alike I can try to find one, but Wilson already knows the script, and I don't think our customer would recognize the real guy if he sat next to him at lunch."

"Speaking of which," Stuarti said, "what *about* lunch? What happens if he gets hungry?"

"Sandwiches on executive china," Eliot responded with unruffled calm, "served out of Office B by the Marines.

We've been bringing the place settings in over the past ten days."

Irked by what he felt to be Eliot's unnecessarily flashy show of competence, Stuarti grumbled sullenly for a moment, then turned and addressed the group.

"Good afternoon, gentlemen," he said. "My name's Stuarti, and I'd like to welcome you to the site rehearsal meeting of the President's Senior Arms Control Policy Group. I've worked with some of you before. The rest of you come with Eliot's highest personal recommendation. You represent the cream of the nation's talent in your field, and I'd like to take this opportunity to say that it's an honor to Big Store with you. Anybody have any trouble getting in?"

No one had.

"Good," Stuarti said, and without further preamble he began. "The Senior Arms Control Policy Group, or Sackpig, as it has happily and inevitably come to be known, was created by the Reagan administration in mid-1983 in an attempt to fill a perceived bureaucratic void between the National Security Council and the Politico-Military Interdepartmental Group, or PMIG. It was hoped at the time that the Sackpig would be able to overcome the endless and inconclusive bickering at the assistant secretary level between the Departments of Defense and State that had largely paralyzed the strategic debate in the early years of the administration. While this hope has yet to be realized, the Sackpig, on paper at least, remains a formidable bureaucratic entity with which codename Bunny is certain to be familiar.

"The departmental composition of the meeting that codename Bunny will attend—assuming the continued forebearance of the Bureau in not yanking the silly bastard off the street—is, as you have perhaps noticed, dominated by the Department of Defense, with only a single, and dissenting, representative from State, and will on that ground give the appearance of a bureaucratic coup by the DOD. The ostensible purpose of the meeting will be to draft, for the president's

119

signature, a National Security Decision Directive expressly defining the administration's policy in regard to arms control, and by extension its policy in regard to the contingent areas of nuclear targeting and weapons development.

"While the technical presentation will largely be conducted by Professor Quade and the under secretary of defense for policy, who," Stuarti added with a venomous glance at Harold, "if he deviates one *iota* from the written script will be instantly removed by the Marines to Office B and have his *nuts* cut off, it was nonetheless thought useful for those others of you with speaking parts to have some advance familiarity with the terms of the debate. To this end, we have asked Professor Quade—an ayatollah, as you all know, among the nuclear warfare mullahs—to address us this afternoon. Professor Quade spoke at the ACDA six months ago to an audience that included our customer, and inasmuch as he all but called for the Agency's dismantling, it's likely that our customer will remember him. Professor, please."

"For those of you who wish to follow in your scripts, people," Eliot sang out, "the agenda appears as Appendix A and Professor Quade's abstract as Appendix F."

To enthusiastic applause from Harold and Bullard, Professor Quade rose to his feet, glancing at Stuarti.

"I had expected to have my charts . . ." he said.

"And so you will, doc," Stuarti said reassuringly. "It's just a summary we're after today."

Arranging his notes on the table before him, Professor Quade straightened and began to speak.

"The case against strategic arms control," he began, "can be made both on historical and technical grounds. While for centuries countries have attempted to devise schemes to limit the means of making war, it is only in the past quarter century that weapons-cutting negotiations have come to dominate the relations between the world's most powerful countries. I shall argue in the meeting that this is an historical anomaly that

120

cannot long endure, indeed, that in a world in which there is no court to adjudicate treaty violations, nor agency to compel compliance with treaty terms, attempts to achieve such treaties are self-deluding folly, inevitably driven not by military but by electoral considerations." Professor Quade paused, looked up, resumed. "I shall base my argument on the following axioms: first, that mutual deterrence—what the newspapers call the balance of terror—is for the foreseeable future the best source of military stability we are likely to find, and second, that it is not the 'balance' of terror—the sheer equality or symmetry of weapons systems—that constitutes mutual deterrence, but rather the *stability* of that balance. The balance is stable, by definition, only when neither side, in striking first, can destroy the adversary's ability to strike back. In other words, *any meaningful arrangement to maintain stability must have as its most important objective the safety of weapons rather than the safety of people.* Let us, in the light of this awareness, examine the contribution of so-called arms control . . ."

"Old Doom turns a dandy apocalyptic phrase, eh?" Stuarti whispered into Bullard's ear.

Bullard primly put his finger to his lips, nodded sternly in the direction of Professor Quade, then folded his hands in his lap and assumed an expression of intense concentration, ignoring Stuarti.

". . . thus, by limiting *launchers* rather than *warheads*, the SALT Treaty encouraged both sides to load as many MIRVs as possible onto as many ICBMs as possible. This, clearly, was doubly destabilizing, creating weapons systems that simultaneously threatened *and* invited a preemptive strike. Similarly, it can be seen in retrospect that the Soviet SS20 missile was consciously designed to take advantage of loopholes in the SALT Treaty, which in turn, for political rather than military reasons, forced upon the NATO alliance the unfortunate 'two-track' decision of 1979, with the resulting and inevitable deployment not only of the Tomahawk and Persh-

121

ing missles, but of additional SS20s. Here, clearly, is yet another instance in which arms control, far from controlling arms, has had the effect of driving the development of new weapons."

"An argument that has been made repeatedly and in public by the assistant secretary of defense for security policy," Stuarti interjected. "This isn't just some fruitcake raving, gentlemen; this is your government talking."

"Theory, I believe," Quade continued with an offended glance at Stuarti, "will help us in understanding these anomalies. Consider an agreement limiting the absolute number of missiles allowed to each side. Let us suppose that we had determined, from a consideration of population targets and enemy incentives, that we would require a minimum of one hundred missiles left over after his preemptive countermissile strike in order to launch an adequately punitive retaliatory strike, that is, to deter his first strike. Let us further suppose the accuracy and reliability of his missiles to be such that one of his has a fifty percent chance of taking out one of ours. Thus, if we have two hundred, he must destroy just over half; at fifty percent reliability he must launch slightly more than two hundred of his own to be certain of cutting our residual supply to less than one hundred. If we had four hundred, he would be obliged to take out three-quarters of ours, thus needing, given the fifty percent discount rate, to fire more than twice four hundred, or more than eight hundred. If we had eight hundred, he would be obliged to destroy more than seven-eighths of ours, and to do so at a fifty percent discount rate he would need over three times that number, or more than twenty-four hundred. In short, gentlemen, the larger the initial number on the 'defending' side, the larger the *multiple* required by the 'attacking' side in order to reduce the defender's residual supply to acceptable levels. Thus, for roughly equal numbers on both sides, the likelihood of a successful counterforce first strike *decreases* as the absolute numbers of missiles on both sides *increase*. Additionally, the *tolerance* of the system is enhanced as well. For small numbers on each side, a ratio of advantage in the neighborhood of two or three to one might permit a 'rational' first strike, whereas with higher initial numbers, it may require a ratio of ten to one rather than two or three to one. Thus neither side needs to panic if it falls behind a bit, and neither can hope to draw sufficiently ahead to achieve effective dominance. Viewed in this perspective, *a limitation on the number of missiles allowed to each side would be more stabilizing, the larger the number permitted . . .*"

Harold moaned aloud.

"Does your script call for moaning?" Stuarti demanded.

"No," Harold admitted, "it's just that . . ."

"Then don't moan," Stuarti snapped. "Please go ahead, doc."

The remaining two points that Professor Quade had to make were simple ones, both deriving from his axiomatic emphasis on crisis stability. First, that countervalue targeting is an inevitable logical complement of the increased awareness of the destabilizing nature of counterforce targeting and technology, and second, that if our aim is to guarantee to an enemy our ability to strike a punitive blow after being struck ourselves, we should find virtue in technological discoveries that enhance the antipopulation potency of our retaliatory weapons. However simple in theory, a lifelong habit of didacticism and the nearly theological language in which the points were couched precluded brevity. By the time Professor Quade droned to a close, the better part of an hour and nearly everyone's hope for the future had been exhausted.

"I should like to thank Professor Quade for his appallingly expert *tour d'horizon*," Stuarti beamed as Quade resumed his seat to an utter absence of applause. "Let me simply say, doc, that if I were our customer, listening to this dreadful nonsense for the first time, I would've already thrown up into my *shoes* with terror."

123

"Just a figure of speech, professor," Bullard interrupted with alarm. "Pay no . . ."

"Let us, however," Stuarti continued inexorably, "leave for a moment the dog food level of our enterprise, and speak to its larger context, which is *art*.

"In art," Stuarti said, "there is a single standing dictum that we must always hold clearly in our minds, particularly you younger artists. It is this: *No forgery can be counted on to last beyond one generation.* The style of the forger, it is felt, like that of the artist, is inescapably permeated by his own generation. In recent years, the most *skilled*, the most *sensitive* of forgers . . ."

"Steady, Ed," Bullard murmured.

". . . or so I am told . . . have with stunning success turned their hands to the reproduction of Coptic art. This is so because the style of Coptic art—forceful, overworked, overstated—is sufficiently consonant with the taste of our own age that the style of the individual forger disappears, as it were, only to emerge a generation or two hence.

"My point, gentlemen, is that what matters in a forgery is not exactitude of reproduction—though Irving will provide the meeting with precise documentation that our customer will have the opportunity to steal, photocopy, or read—nor are we overly concerned with theoretical error or inconsistency. Indeed, inconsistency can be construed, these parlous days, as a mark of genuineness. What we *are* concerned with is the *matrix* in which both documentation and error will be encountered, and of this matrix we shall ask only this question: *Is it in the style of its time?* Our interest is not in forging documents, although there will be forged documents. Nor is it in selling flawed ideas, which, like Dr. Doom's supply-side arms control—" Bullard glared "—we have in rich plenty. Our interest, in short, is to forge an *impression*, which, like all impressions, will of necessity be ephemeral. If we are successful, our customer, when he leaves this room, will do so believing himself to have been present at a meeting of the president's Senior Arms Control Policy Group, in the course of which *the abandonment of arms control in favor of an open-ended arms race, the development of 'dirty' nuclear weapons, and the deliberate targeting of enemy civilian population centers will have been ratified as this nation's policy.* Any questions?"

Professor Quade raised his hand.

"Yes, professor?"

"As a scientist," Professor Quade said in a tone of measured pomposity, "I have already registered my personal reservations at being asked to participate in a deliberate campaign of what I believe you call disinformation . . ."

"That's what we call it, doc," Stuarti agreed cheerfully.

"As a strategical theorist," Quade continued, ignoring Stuarti, "I should further like to assert, without qualification, my opinion that the disinformation that it is the function of this group to implant is of such a nature that while it might seem plausible, even compelling, to the lay mind, it will not bear even a relatively cursory expert evaluation. In short, gentlemen, the Soviets *will not believe this information,* however elaborate its provenance. I have made this point time and again, and time and again I have been rebuffed by the brain trust responsible for the script. I should feel remiss not to voice this objection one final time."

"On behalf of the brain trustees, doc," Stuarti said generously, "I'd like to commend you for your unrelenting candor. Any other questions?"

"Perhaps I haven't made myself clear," Quade said with irritation. "Let me try once more. An expert would suspect disinformation, no matter the quality of the supporting documentation, within seventy-two hours."

The serenity with which Stuarti received this observation was startling enough. It was his reply, however, which, when cited in the years to come in those secret precincts where the case was reanalyzed and discussed, lent lustre to his legend and substance to the claim that he had, from the earliest moments of the case, perceived the outline of all that was to come.

"Seventy-two hours," Stuarti said, "should be just about enough."

CHAPTER SIXTEEN

THEN waiting was all there was to do, and waiting was difficult for everyone.

Stuarti, temperamentally disinclined to inactivity, passed the days sullenly slumped in his wheelchair, watching the fish die and urging his Mormon to polygamy while awaiting the twice daily phone call from Matthews.

Minihan each morning delivered to the townhouse the surveillance logs, photos, and tape concordances documenting Bunny's activities of the previous twenty-four hours and daily warned Stuarti of the gathering consensus at alarmingly senior levels of Federal Counterintelligence that Bunny's proper place was in a cell, rather than on a leash, however short.

It was for Matthews, however, passing the days dispensing towels and advice at the Twelfth Street gym and the nights in sleepless longing on his cot in the room on Sullivan Street, that the waiting was very nearly unbearable, and by the evening of the fifth day, when the waiting finally ended, Matthews was riding a high, thin edge of anger that, in an agent of his own, he would instantly have recognized as dangerously inappropriate.

* * *

The gym was open from noon 'til nine, and Matthews later assumed that his deliberately punctual comings and goings had been previously observed, for it was 8:50 that Wednesday evening when, from the far end of the gym where for the third evening in a row he was unsuccessfully attempting to teach a florist to skip rope, he heard the schoolmaster's bell on the entrance desk ring and looked down the length of the room into the smiling face and expressionless eyes of Priscilla No-Last-Name.

"Hi!" she said brightly as Matthews approached. "Remember me? I'm the girl you left living the clean life last week."

Matthews crossed to the window and looked carefully into the street. He then looked behind him to where the florist, the gym's single customer at that hour, was dangling from the horizontal bar, kicking furiously in lieu of a pull-up, and only then did he look squarely at Priscilla and speak.

"What do you want?" he demanded, unsmiling.

"I'd like to talk to Markie, actually," she said. "Assuming people can still talk to Markie without a ouija board."

"I don't know a Markie," Matthews said.

"Sure you do," Priscilla continued with a breezy confidence that underscored rather than masked her nervousness. "The guy that introduced us. The guy you beat the shit out of in my apartment last week. The guy you took away and that nobody's seen since."

Ignoring the florist, Matthews put the flat of his left hand against Priscilla's chest and pushed her firmly back against the towel locker where he held her as, unhurriedly and without speech, he searched her body with his right hand, running it beneath her blouse and deep inside the waistband of her jeans, front and back.

"You must be a real surprise on a first date," Priscilla said, licking her lips as Matthews, having satisfied himself that she was not wired, straightened and spoke again.

128

"What do you want?" he repeated.

"Like I told you," she said. "I wanna talk to Markie. In fact, *lots* of people seem to want to talk to Markie. The cops, for instance, want to talk to him so bad that they kicked in his door last Friday night. About fifteen of 'em, I understand. No Markie, though. I thought maybe you could help me. Unless, of course, you'd rather help the cops, you bein' the last person to see him and everything."

"Are you threatening me?" Matthews asked quietly.

"No, no," she said with a smile so bright and inappropriate that Matthews assumed its chief ingredient to be listed in the Merck Manual. "It's just that you bein' on parole and everything, I thought maybe you'd rather talk to me than them. I mean, I don't *care* or anything, I'd just like to know, y'know? Is Markie dead?"

Matthews regarded her carefully for a moment before he spoke, as though deciding which answer would serve him best.

"No," he said.

"You're lying," she said cheerfully. "I can tell."

"How?" asked Matthews, feigning amusement, poorly.

"I've got a friend who's killed some people," she said, her smile undimmed, "and he's got eyes just like yours."

"He's myopic?" Matthews asked, smiling and repressing a shudder.

"You'd kill me, too, wouldn't you?" Priscilla continued with a giggle. "If you could be sure that I hadn't told somebody I was coming to see you, and that you might."

"Did you?" Matthews asked.

"You fuckin' bet," the girl beamed.

"There're a lot of people out there with glasses," Matthews said uneasily. "I don't want to spoil your gypsy routine or anything, but I'm afraid you've got a wrong number."

The radio in the gym was blaring rock music, and for a moment the girl closed her eyes and hummed along, her fingers snapping softly and her hips stirring to the music. Still dancing, she opened her eyes and smiled as she spoke.

129

"Well," she said, "*I* don't believe you, but maybe the cops will. 'Course they don't know shit about eyes."

"Listen," Matthews said, an edge of anger and urgency creeping into his voice. "Markie did something wrong, and now he's going to get a chance to do something right, make it all better. The problem is, is that Markie's got a big mouth, and so until he does it, he stays on ice. A week from now, you can talk to him all you like. Of course, I'm not real sure that he wants to talk to you. He's all pissed off, claims that you threw him over for the Mad Bomber or some bullshit like that, and I think he might rather play catch-up than have a chat."

"C'mon, c'mon," Priscilla smiled reprovingly. "He told you that fairy story when he was still lying on the floor at my place, puking. Listen," she said, doodling with her finger in the sweat on Matthews's chest, "I'd like to believe you. Hard guys turn me on, and I think we might have a good time with each other, you 'n me. But if you *want* me to believe you, you're gonna hafta do a whole lot better'n that."

Matthews looked the smiling girl up and down, breathed deeply, sighed.

"All right," he said finally. "How about if you talk to him on the phone, hear his voice. *Then* will you believe he's alive?"

Priscilla's smile remained in place, but for an instant, like a wisp of cloud blown across a brilliant sun, another emotion passed briefly and almost unnoticeably across her features, whether fear or anticipation Matthews could not tell.

"Yes," she said after a moment. "If I can talk to him, and he can talk back and everything, I suppose I'd hafta figure he's alive. Call him."

"Not from here," Matthews said flatly. "I work here."

"Then where're we gonna call from?" she asked carefully.

"It doesn't make any difference to me," Matthews shrugged. "Bar, pay phone, whatever. Just not here."

"I suppose we could call from my place," she said, her

130

smile now frankly one of invitation and her spontaneity almost convincing. "It's got a phone. *And* a bed."

"I suppose we could," Matthews said, smiling back for the first time since she had entered.

Reaching past her, Matthews opened the cash drawer of the desk, removed a quarter, and turned to the pay phone on the wall.

"What are you doing?" she asked uncertainly.

"I've got to make another call," Matthews said easily. "And then I've got to take a shower. You want a Coke or anything, there's some change in the drawer."

"No calls," she said firmly, but her voice lacked the authority with which the instruction had been given her. Matthews did not even bother to turn as he spoke, still dialing.

"Listen, sweetheart," he said. "If talking to Weinstein is going to make you feel better and get you out of my hair, you can talk to Weinstein. Whatever else I do is my own goddamned business. . . . Yeah," he said as the phone was answered, "is Darlene there?"

"No," Stuarti said grumpily and without hesitation. "She's out. You want to leave a message or anything?"

"Yeah," Matthews said. "Tell her Norris called. Tell her I can't make it tonight and that I'll call her tomorrow at work."

"She should be in soon," Stuarti said. "You want her to call you?"

"Sure, if she comes in," Matthews said. "I'll be at the gym for another ten minutes or so. She's got the number. Tell her to let it ring, I'll be in the shower. Otherwise, I'll talk to her tomorrow."

In his indifference, Stuarti did not even say good-bye as he hung up.

It was 9:15 when Matthews emerged from the men's locker room, wearing running shoes, a faded pair of jeans, and a poplin windbreaker. The gym was empty, Matthews having

131

locked the door behind the florist and extinguished the outside
lights before bathing, and Priscilla No-Last-Name was perched
sulkily on the Nautilus chest machine, reading *People* magazine and smoking a joint.

"No Darlene," she said brightly when he came out.

"There's always a Darlene," Matthews said. "Come here."

Taking a last drag on the joint, Priscilla dropped the roach
onto the carpet, ground it out with her foot, and sauntered
to where Matthews stood.

"Feel this lump?" he asked.

The girl reached out her hand and touched him.

"Yes," she said.

"The other lump," Matthews said, raising her hand to his
waist and pressing it against his jacket.

"It's a gun," she said.

"That's right," Matthews said. "And if you're setting me
up for some of Markie's friends, a lot of people are gonna
get shot and you're going to be one of them."

"Well," the girl said, the fixed brightness of her smile suggesting that the joint had only been a chaser, "I appreciate
your being up-front and everything, but Markie didn't really
have too many friends. Customers, y'know, but not friends."

As they stepped into the street, Matthews locking the door
and activating the alarm system behind them, the darkness
and the fear struck him, simultaneously, as sharply as a slap,
for he was reasonably certain that if the girl did not believe
that Weinstein was alive, they would never make it as far as
her apartment.

In the shadowed doorway, the girl put her arms around
Matthews's waist and pulled him tightly against her, leaning
back and smiling into his face.

"Hey," she said, as though proposing an idea that had just
occurred to her. "Let's walk, get a little exercise."

"Whatever you like," Matthews said, smiling back his
nausea and stroking her breasts lingeringly, wishing, as he
did so, that he could be certain that it was desire, and

not some darker excitement, that brought her nipples up so quickly.

Although he could not identify Stuarti's cars and vans and pavement teams, the twenty-minute lead time that he had given Stuarti made it certain that they were there, and allowed Matthews to assure himself that if, indeed, someone shot him along the way, the shooter would have company to the number forty before the echo died, if not before he did.

As Matthews and the girl strolled beneath the marquee of the Greenwich Cinema and turned toward Seventh Avenue, a pair of lovers emerged from the Village Den restaurant across the street, the man's arm around the girl's shoulder and their heads together.

"That was yummy," sighed the girl, giving her swain a peck.

"They've left the gym, heading south on Greenwich Avenue," the man smiled back, addressing his remark, it seemed, more nearly to the woman's collar than to her ear.

"Roger," said the collar tightly, in a voice very like Stuarti's, as beneath the sidewalk gratings a subway rumbled, briefly flooding the night air with a fetid stink of electricity, rotting paper, and popcorn. *"Stay close."*

Which was sound advice, for as Matthews and Priscilla No-Last-Name passed the cinema and turned toward Seventh Avenue a straw-haired man wearing a navy track suit and Adidas running shoes detached himself from the ticket line and drifted east on Twelfth, eating an apple, toward the emergency room entrance of St. Vincent's hospital.

Though he knew from the girl's embrace where Matthews and the girl were headed, the East German knew just then no more than Matthews whether the gun dealer Norris— whose identity as a recent parolee from Green Haven Prison the credit agency had confirmed with a contact in the parole administration—would be returned to that same emergency room within the hour, if only to have his death certified, as required by law.

133

But he *would* know.

Soon.

Though the formal record would later insist that their walk to East Sixth Street took only forty-eight minutes, to Matthews, wondering what her signal was to be, its duration seemed more nearly that of a human lifetime.

From the gym at Greenwich and Twelfth to the east side of Seventh Avenue Priscilla held his right arm in both hands, her head against his shoulder. Diverted by a remainder table at the Idle Hour Bookstore, she insisted on browsing for a few minutes, and when they resumed their walk it was his left arm that she held.

Before crossing Sixth Avenue at Ninth Street, she removed her shoes, dangling them carelessly over her shoulder in one hand, and the thirty seconds that they spent window-shopping at Balducci's, their backs naked to both pedestrian and automobile traffic, were perhaps the longest thirty seconds of Matthews's life.

At Fifth Avenue and Washington Square North, where Priscilla, reporting herself tired of dodging dog shit in the dark, replaced her shoes, they were accosted by a drunk emerging from the park to panhandle. Rebuffed, the drunk cursed Matthews and followed them for a step or two before a second glance from Matthews discouraged further speech. Silently, he watched them walk away, and it was only when they were safely a block distant that he hitched up his pants and shouted a final obscenity; a tactical delay which, in retrospect, was judged fortunate indeed, for had he gone to his pocket a moment sooner the passenger in a blue van behind him marked Decker's Cleaners would have cut him in half with an Ithaca pump gun.

Finally, on Seventh Street east of the Bowery, there was a moment of pure terror as, without a word, the girl released his arm and dropped from sight between two parked cars, but she was only peeing, and when she stood and zipped her pants her smile seemed to Matthews less tightly clenched, and he guessed that they had already walked past the gun, perhaps in the crowd around Balducci's, where a subsonic round through a small suppressor would have been no more noticeable, save in its effect, than a cough.

In the hallway of her tenement on East Sixth Street, Priscilla watched with lively curiosity as Matthews unzipped his windbreaker and removed the handgun from his belt. Wordlessly, no explanation seeming necessary, he then took the girl by the hair and held her firmly in front of him, and with the muzzle of the pistol pressed against her spine they ascended the stairs together, the only sound the shuffle of their footsteps and the girl's strained panting.

Nothing exploded when she unlocked the door, and when she turned on the light Matthews shoved her hard before him, sending her sprawling onto the apartment floor, and entered behind her, fast, his gun braced in both hands sweeping the empty room.

The bathroom, too, as Priscilla at his terse instruction slowly opened the door, was empty.

"Satisfied?" she asked sulkily, rubbing her left knee.

"Nothing personal," Matthews said. "I just had to be sure."

"Feel me up, pull my hair, knock me down," the girl said. "It's like bein' in fuckin' sixth grade again. You gonna call Markie, or what?"

"If I do," Matthews said, "you stay away from the cops, right? Keeping in mind that I'm not the only one in this, and if I end up in the joint, you end up in the *ground*."

"You got a deal," the girl said, smiling again. "I just want to know if he's alive, is all."

"You got a drink?" Matthews asked, waiting to begin to dial until she crossed to the table and poured him a Cognac from a new magnum of Remy Martin.

Again Stuarti answered, this time restraining himself until the third ring.

"Hello, Eddie?" Matthews said. "It's me. Hey, listen, I had

a visit at the gym tonight from Weinstein's girlfriend . . . I don't know, I think probably she heard him say . . . no, no problem, I'm with her now. She wants to make sure he's alive, is all. . . ." Matthews laughed. "Got me, maybe he owes her money. You think maybe you could put him on the phone, tell him to say hello or whatever? . . . Sure, and if he says anything he's not supposed to, give him a crack in the head."

Matthews covered the phone with his hand and spoke to the girl, giving Stuarti what he desperately hoped would be sufficient time to patch him through to the military facility at St. Alban's, Queens, where Weinstein was being held.

"Here's how it works," he said. "You don't ask him where he is, and you don't ask him what he's going to do. Also no names, and no days of the week. Got it?"

"Yes," the girl said.

Matthews again raised the receiver to his ear. "Hello?" he said.

"Hello?"

Weinstein's voice was as clear as if he were speaking from next door, and no tighter than one would expect it to be given the fact of Koko's hand on his throat.

Matthews handed the receiver to the girl.

"Markie?" the girl said. "Yeah, it's me. You OK, an' everything?"

Sitting beside the girl, Matthews could hear Weinstein's voice, high-pitched and climbing, though he could not make out the words. For a moment the girl listened silently, then without speaking further replaced the receiver in its cradle.

"That was short," Matthews said.

"It was Markie, too," the girl said quietly. "You're right, he's alive."

"What'd he say?" Matthews asked.

The girl crossed the room to a small refrigerator, took out a Coca-Cola, and turned to Matthews, smiling.

"He said that I should go fuck myself," she said brightly. "I guess he must have forgotten that you were here."

136

Opening a small cloisonné box on the table, the girl removed two folded pieces of paper, each the size and shape of a stick of chewing gum.

"You want some?"

"What is it?" Matthews asked.

"Speedball," the girl said. "You'll like it."

"No thanks," Matthews said. "There were guys in the joint, told themselves they were just playing around with smack, and ended up with a fat new habit to feed. I'll stick with this."

Matthews drained his Cognac, stood, and poured himself another. As he watched, the girl carefully unfolded one of the pieces of paper, tilted her head, and closing one nostril with her finger inhaled the quarter-teaspoonful of white powder that it held.

For a moment she closed her eyes, breathing once the word "Jesus." When again she opened them and smiled, her pupils were so dilated that her eyes seemed black.

"Party time," she said, unbuttoning her blouse and shrugging it from her shoulders, and Matthews, who very much needed a plausible reason to return and had thus no choice to make at all, could only wonder briefly why impotence, like faith, was never there when one needed it most.

It was shortly after four in the morning when Matthews emerged from the tenement building into the stillness of East Sixth Street. The static watchers in a van at the corner recorded the precise time as 4:07 A.M., also recording, as per Stuarti's instructions and with some alarm, the fact that while walking to the corner of Avenue C to hail a cab Matthews suddenly paused, put his hands on his knees, and there waited for a moment, as though he feared he might vomit.

The East German, too, watching from a second-floor window of an abandoned building halfway up the block, noted Matthews's spasm of nausea, attributing it to drink or drugs. The girl's signal in front of the store had been unambiguous:

Weinstein was alive, and Norris the gun dealer knew where he was. That Weinstein had not come that evening was disappointing, but only a temporary inconvenience. If Norris had felt obliged to placate the girl that evening, he would feel so obliged again, whenever she insisted, and the next time he would talk to Norris himself. Bending, he replaced the heavy pistol that had rested on the windowsill in an attaché case at his feet, noting with distaste as he did so the acrid smell of his own sweat.

It was only the driver of the gypsy cab that returned him to the room on Sullivan Street, however—glancing in the rearview mirror when Matthews failed to respond to a pleasantry—who noticed that his passenger, soundlessly and without touching his face, was weeping.

CHAPTER SEVENTEEN

"SO you think it was just a dry run, then?" Stuarti asked, pouring a slug of Dewar's into his coffee and waggling the bottle at Matthews, who declined.

"No," said Matthews, stepping away from the window from which he had been watching the morning commuters hurrying to the subway, and allowing Stuarti's Mormon to draw the curtains in preparation for Minihan's slide show. "She wanted to walk, and led the whole way. I suspect that somewhere along the line she walked me past Andreas, and if she could have been sure that Weinstein was dead, I would have been, too."

"That must have been an odd feeling," Stuarti remarked mildly, but Matthews, watching Minihan load slides into a carousel, was disinclined, it seemed, to talk about odd feelings.

"Were you able to make the signal that she used?" Stuarti asked.

"Her shoes, I think," Matthews said. "She seemed to relax a bit once she got them on again. Could've just been relief at not having to worry about dog shit and broken glass though. When are the pictures going to be ready?"

"What did they say, Frank?" Stuarti asked. "About noon?"

"We're talking about some fifteen hundred frames," Minihan said. "We should have the first batch around eleven or so, and the rest by three. Call it four, by the time they get them out to Weinstein."

"How's the quality going to be?" Matthews asked.

"Good," Minihan said. "They used some new night film. Everything's going to be a little green, but they shouldn't be grainy at all, even where there's movement."

"Tell them to start Weinstein on the blocks between Sixth Avenue and Ninth Street and Waverly and University," Matthews said. "And make sure he goes over every frame with a hand-held glass. I want check marks above every face, and computer enhancements for any question marks. And not just male pedestrians, either. Bag ladies, cops, Good Humor men, *everybody*. Tell him he wins a review copy of Gerald Ford's *A Time to Heal* and early parole if he makes the face."

"All we've got him on is possession of narcotics," Minihan objected, "and we're seventy-two hours past the post for arraignment on *that*. I don't think he's going to have to worry about early parole."

"Then tell him we won't kill him," Matthews snapped, and when Minihan, startled, paused and looked up, the pale blue eyes behind Matthews's glasses made the obverse suddenly seem a chillingly real possibility.

"So you think she'll be back?" Stuarti interrupted hurriedly.

"With Weinstein alive and babbling about Mad Bombers?" Matthews said. "She'll be back. He'll send her as soon as he's ready to make his move. I imagine she'll ask me to her apartment."

"Why?" Stuarti demanded.

"In his place," shrugged Matthews, "I'd kill all three of us, too. Wouldn't you?"

"No, no," Stuarti said, shaking his head and shuddering.

"What will she use as an excuse to ask you back? She already knows that Weinstein's alive."

"She doesn't need an excuse," Matthews said. "We made friends."

"Yes?" Stuarti looked up with bright curiosity.

"Yes," said Matthews, flatly.

"Any guess when?" Stuarti asked.

"Soon," Matthews said. "Tomorrow, day after. Andreas needs Weinstein dead yesterday, and I'm the one who knows where he is."

"Today?" Stuarti asked.

"Nope," said Matthews. "Today's my day off at the gym, and that's where she'll call me. I'd like to give Weinstein a crack at the pictures, anyway. It'd be handy knowing what the guy I'm supposed to shoot looks like."

The strain in Matthews's voice seemed to be catching, for it was only with difficulty that Stuarti maintained his normal tone when he spoke.

"The reason that I ask, dear boy," Stuarti said, "is that we seem to be running out of time."

"Why?" Matthews asked.

"Because the bureau's made Bunny's contact," Stuarti said. "You about ready, Frank?"

"Yes," Minihan said thoughtfully, gazing at Matthews for a moment before nodding to Stuarti's Mormon, who extinguished the lights.

For a moment there was darkness broken only by a blinding beam of white light illuminating the blank projection screen, then, with a soft click, there was a photo of a woman.

She was fair-haired and fortyish, wore a tweed skirt and a brown wool cardigan wrapped around her shoulders, and was waiting for the light to change at the corner of Fifth Avenue and Sixty-second Street. The picture had been taken from a car, Matthews noticed, the right B post of which cropped the left border of the photo.

"Mary D. Berg," Minihan said. "British passport, forty-six years old, single. Head of operations for the New York office of Simpson's Tours of London. Works in Rockefeller Center."

With another soft click, the first picture was replaced by a second. The woman was descending the steps into Central Park at Sixty-third Street, carrying, Matthews noted from habit, a shopping bag from Saks.

"Impressive employment record," Minihan continued. "Started as a booking agent in the London office in 1963. From '63 to '72 she beavered away in London, working days in the back office at Simpson's and taking night courses in data processing. She was active in the design of a lot of their initial systems, and supervised the cutover from their paper base in 1970. In 1973 they made her assistant head of operations in the London office."

"A computer expert," Stuarti said, to no one in particular.

"And the indispensable employee," added Minihan.

Another click, and the woman had entered the zoo and was standing, rapt, before the Barbary goats.

"Then she began to travel," Minihan said. "Head of operations, Tokyo office, 1975 to '78. Operations again, Munich office, 1978 to '80. She's been in New York since May of '81."

The carousel advanced another frame, and the woman was feeding the pigeons in front of the zebras.

"She plays bridge, keeps two corgis, and has a photo portrait of the queen mother over her mantle," Minihan said. "Before she was posted overseas, she bought a small flat in Hampstead, which she still maintains. Neighbors say she keeps to herself, save for volunteer work for the RSPCA and the CND."

"The Campaign for Nuclear Disarmament?" Matthews said.

"Sure," said Minihan. "Why not? Resist American hegemonism and keep the world safe for the corgis of tomorrow.

142

Almost a moral duty. Damned eloquent about it, too. We've got her on tape, and when she gets going about 'mankind's obligation to save itself from the follies of statesmen,' well, it's hard not to be moved. *Particularly* for Bunny. They argue, they weep, they come to consensus, they take their pants off . . ."

"You've got them together on tape?" Matthews demanded.

"Sure," Minihan said. "We've got his place spiked with snorkel probes. The last contact was three weeks ago, and absolutely nothing since. Two days before Butterfield died somebody decided to tighten up the field rules, *hard*. I *can* report from the earlier tape, however, that the woman is nowhere near as repressed as she looks."

Another click, and another photo of the Berg woman, her back to the camera, leaning against the railing of the seal pond.

"Of course," Minihan said, "she's also not as *English* as she looks. Turns out Ms. Berg is a naturalized subject, who immigrated to the U.K. from Graz, Austria in 1956. Plenty of room, then, in England's green and pleasant land, for orphans and refugees, particularly little girls." Minihan paused. "That is, of course, if you count sixteen as a little girl. In those days sixteen was pretty well grown up, particularly in the Eastern sector, from which she entered Austria as a refugee in late 1955. The records are still there."

"Go ahead," Matthews said, his voice tired.

"Marya Dimitriovna Berg," Minihan said quietly. "Born August, 1940, at Dnepropetrovsk, in the Ukraine. According to immigration records, her parents died in 1943. Raised by an alcoholic uncle, who abused her. Grew up, and lit out for the West first chance she got. A courageous little tyke."

"Any of it true?" asked Matthews.

"Yes," Stuarti said, when Minihan paused. "We actually sent a Ukrainian of ours to Dnepropetrovsk, which wasn't easy because it's in a restricted zone. Sure enough, the birth records were there, corroborating her statements to Austrian Immigration. I'm afraid the orphan part's a little shaky, though."

"Yes?" Matthews said.

"Yes," said Stuarti. "Her mother still lives there. By herself in a *two-bedroom* apartment. Does her shopping at the *beriozki*, too."

"Beriozki?" Minihan asked.

"Foreign currency stores," said Matthews, absently. "Strictly for party officials and their families. And KGB, of course."

Minihan again advanced the carousel. In the foreground, the Berg woman, blurred, was visible still watching the seals, but the focus of the photo was on the terrace above, where a small crowd had gathered to watch the gorillas.

"Bunny," Stuarti said softly. "To the right, by the Sabrett cart."

"I've got him," Matthews said. "And even though I can't see the front of his shopping bag, I'd be willing to bet it's from Saks."

"You'd win your bet," Minihan said. "I'll run through these next frames quickly, shall I?"

As Minihan began to do so, the only sounds in the room were the clicking of the slide projector and Stuarti's breathing. With the jerky, truncated movement of a figure in an early motion picture, the Berg woman slowly circled the concrete pond, her attention held by the keeper, who, with a bucket of fish at his feet, was preparing to feed the seals. As the crowd began to gather, Bunny drifted down from the upper terrace and joined its fringe. By the time the first fish was thrown he was standing next to Mary Berg, and when it was fielded cleanly on the fly by the senior seal, Bunny, a sheepish grin confessing the little boy in him still, was, like Mary Berg, sufficiently delighted to put his shopping bag down and join in the general applause.

Though the crowd was riveted on the performance, the camera only had eyes for the two shopping bags, and when

144

the feeding was over and the crowd began to disperse, Bunny and the woman having shared neither a glance nor a word, there was no doubt at all that each departed with the other's bag.

No one spoke as Minihan turned off the projector and gestured to Stuarti's Mormon to open the curtains.

"So much for Bunny's contact," Stuarti said finally, as though waiting for someone else to speak. "How close are you to the case officer who services Berg?"

"I think we've already got him on film," Minihan said. "Some fat older guy who has to be the world's worst dresser. Wears wool suits that end just below the knee, and white socks. We call him Spats. We've got him with her in front of the Plaza, twice, and both times we've lost him in the General Motors Building. If he's the guy, it's only a matter of a day or two, and believe me, Ed, as soon as the FCI boys in the Bureau think they've got enough to go, they're going to grab them all. Your time's running out."

"Do what you can," Stuarti said wearily. "We need all the . . ."

"Bunny's a Willie," Matthews said, and his voice was so distant that he might have been speaking to himself.

"Could be," Stuarti said shortly. "Who cares?"

"What's a Willie?" Minihan asked, sighing.

"Agency jargon," Stuarti snapped. "Refers to an agent whose principal is a false-flagger."

"What?" said Minihan.

"An agent who doesn't know who he's working for," Matthews explained, not looking up from the floor. "Someone who's led by his principal to believe that he's working for a newspaper columnist, or a credit agency, or as a volunteer for the FBI . . ."

"Or, say," Minihan said slowly, "as a concerned citizen cooperating with the Campaign for Nuclear Disarmament."

"Why not?" Matthews said. "Keep the world safe for corgis and get laid at the same time."

"*Or,*" Stuarti said angrily, "someone's offered him a hundred grand, a nice house on the Kutuzovsky Prospekt, and his very own collection of Dean Reed records. I mean, we wouldn't want to forget *that* possibility."

"But you don't believe it," Matthews said, looking squarely at Stuarti. "That's why you've been calling him a silly bastard all along."

"Oh, for Christ's sake," Stuarti said disgustedly.

"That would also explain the appalling tradecraft," Matthews continued. "Two murders on U.S. soil, the use of illegals and lunatics to cover his back, and *still* he manages to get himself caught inside ten months. That pathetic nonsense in the zoo was probably *his* idea. What's she going to say? 'That's not the way we're taught to do it, dearie'? The Willie hypothesis fits the nature of his production, too. Of his two confirmed products, one had to do with an American violation of the SALT II Accords, and the other with the development of a destabilizing offensive weapons system. Both, surely, could be construed as ideologically motivated . . ."

"Fine," Stuarti snapped. "Maybe he's a Willie. And maybe Judas would have felt more comfortable if he'd thought he was working for the *Jerusalem Post* rather than the Romans. Who cares?"

"Are they paying him?" Minihan asked. "Or is he a volunteer? Do we know?"

"Of course," Stuarti said. "They're paying him an arm and a leg."

"How?"

"Four deposits totaling seventy thousand dollars over the past year to a numbered account in Zurich's Handelsbank," Stuarti said firmly. "Two withdrawals, one from the Zurich office and one from the branch in the tax-free zone at Gatwick, both dates corresponding to a trip Bunny took last February."

"How can you know that?" Minihan demanded.

When Stuarti, sulking, did not respond, Matthews spoke.

"Because both the deposits and the withdrawals were made by our side," Matthews explained quietly. "If you have access to someone's travel records, it's not too hard to back-date a corresponding paper trail." Matthews turned again to Stuarti. "Why is it so important to you that Bunny look like some four-square, red-toothed Soviet hood instead of the pathetic little jerk that he is? Why are you so worried that someone might feel sorry for him?"

"This sounds like an editorial conference at *Psychology Today*," Stuarti said, with great disgust, "and I'll be god-damned if I'm going to miss 'Mr. Rogers' in order to listen to a lot of speculative nonsense about Bunny's motivation," and it was only later that Matthews reflected that Stuarti had declined to answer the question. "Let me play you a little chunk of unambiguous reality, nothing speculative about it. I don't believe you've heard this before."

Wheeling his chair to the coffee table, Stuarti picked up a small tape recorder and depressed the Play button.

The sounds that followed were as horrific as they had been the first time, the agony in the girl's whispers as poignant as though someone were beating her, or as though someone, perhaps, were breaking her hands. By the time she finally whispered, "Oh! Lookit, Grandma!" and slipped mercifully to death, Matthews's face was pale and clammy and his hands, gripping his knees, were white at the knuckles and nails.

"Any questions?" Stuarti asked briskly.

"No," said Matthews, his voice tight.

"Good," Stuarti said. "That girl was gutted and Butterfield had his head blown off in order that Bunny could go on playing 'I Spy' with his new girlfriend and still sleep tight at night. He might not know about the girl, but he sure as hell knows about Butterfield. He's made his choice, and he can damn well . . . what are you doing?"

"I'm leaving," Matthews said, standing and brushing his

hands together as if he had sand on them. "If all we've got left is pep talks, you guys can go ahead without me. Mind if I take that tape?"

The hand that Matthews extended was shaking badly, a fact that he did nothing to mask, as though challenging Stuarti or Minihan to remark on it.

"Of course, dear boy," Stuarti said, handing Matthews the recorder. "Where are you going?"

"I'm not sure," Matthews said stiffly. "It's my day off, after all, and the sky's the limit. The laundromat seems like a strong possibility right now, but who knows? I'll call."

"Have a bite to eat and get some sleep," Stuarti said anxiously. "If you don't think you can sleep I've got something you can . . ."

Shaking his head once, Matthews turned and left.

Neither Stuarti nor Minihan spoke as the door closed behind him, and in the extended silence the only sound was that of Stuarti's Mormon, gathering the cups.

Finally Minihan spoke.

"Your ferret's going nuts," he said.

For a long moment Stuarti, slumped in his chair, did not respond, and when at last he spoke his voice was tight with emotion.

"Not on my shift," he said thickly, and as he wheeled himself heavily to the window Minihan was shocked to see that Stuarti's eyes, above pouches of fatigue as dark as bruises, were bright with tears.

CHAPTER EIGHTEEN

THE sun was brilliant, the sky was azure, and the semicircle of children clustered around Kate in short right field was hushed.

Gino, the groundskeeper, had cut the field that morning, and on the grass before them was a baby rabbit that had, Kate guessed, been betrayed by instinct into immobility at the approaching clatter of the gang mower. The little rabbit was still alive, gathered neatly on itself, unmoving. Though its eyes were bright, it did not look at the children nearby, but rather stared fixedly at the unattainable wetlands beyond, vivid with wildflowers and purple spikes of loosestrife, only the light and constant tremor of its body betraying the effort of ignoring them.

While the baby's immobility was comfortably construed by the children as a function of friendliness rather than of spinal injury, there was simply no escaping the fact that it had a cut on its little nose, and no mother to hug it, and as curiosity gave way to empathy emotions began to run high.

It was Herbert Bevis, an eight-year-old from Hawthorne Cottage, who, through his tears, first saw Matthews. Though Herbert was portly, and normally not fleet of foot, he was out of the blocks quickly, and benefiting from the urgency of

149

grief and a ten-yard head start was the first to reach the haven of Matthews's arms.

Barely pausing in his stride, Matthews bent and caught Herbert on the fly, swinging the child up and hugging him close as Herbert, clinging fiercely with arms and legs, confided his grief brokenly to Matthews's neck. Herbert's companions, equally stirred by the sudden and providential appearance of a daddy, were not far behind, and as they returned to Kate, Herbert proudly riding and the other children clinging to the fingers of Matthews's free hand, Kate felt her throat swell with love and pride, and a sudden, piercing longing for a child of their own.

Borrowing a Kleenex from Kate, who carried them in industrial quantity, Matthews knelt, and soothing the baby rabbit with that gentleness noticed only by small children in large men, cleaned the blood from its nose. He then scooped it up softly in his hands, covering with his foot, as he did so, the thick patch of darker blood that remained on the grass beneath.

When everyone had petted the bunny, and assured it of his love, Matthews gently explained that it must now be returned to the woods, where its mother, surely frantic with worry, could find it and care for it. Together he and the children walked to the edge of the field, the baby rabbit sniffing at Matthews's fingers with fearless and vivid interest, the promiscuity of imminent death already upon it.

At the field's edge the children halted, knowing, as they did to the heart, that where daddies went no one followed, and when Matthews at length emerged from the wood the day was again merely glorious, and the air newly sweet.

"Snack!" Kate announced, pointing to the picnic table behind the backstop, and the children fled in a joyous rush, death routed by appetite.

Smiling, Kate turned to Matthews. "That's country living for you," she said, "Franciscan interludes punctuated by graham crackers. Did you have to . . ."

And then she saw his face, and was instantly struck dumb with terror. His skin was colorless, and beaded everywhere with sweat.

His broad hands were open, sticky with blood, and the intensity with which he stared at them was such that, for a terrible moment, Kate feared that he might never stop.

"My God!" she cried. "What's the matter?"

With an effort that hurt her to watch, Matthews slowly closed his hands into fists, hiding the blood, and raised his eyes to hers.

"I'm a little tired," he said, struggling desperately against whatever held him. "I haven't slept."

"Oh, Tom!" she said. "Tell me! Please talk to me! What's wrong?"

"I slept with a woman last night," he said, the words torn from him as though they were gobbets of his own flesh. "And tomorrow I may have to shoot a man in order that we can hang another. But today's my day off . . ."

Here his shaking forced him to pause.

"That's *good*," Kate said brightly, with the desperation of a bystander at a terrible accident who knows no first aid. "You can sleep . . ."

". . . and so I didn't think I'd have to kill anything at all . . ."

"Louise!" Kate called to the monitor, as Matthews turned from her and bent, his breath whistling in his teeth. "Take the children, please! I have to go home."

The call from Hobbes in archives, with whom Stuarti had lingered for a moment at the close of the site rehearsal, came at four that afternoon.

"Where?" Stuarti asked.

"Connecticut," Hobbes said, unable to disguise the pride in his voice. "That's what took so long. New York and New Jersey are easy, but in Connecticut deeds registration is done by township, and between Addison and Woodtick there're

151

two hundred and twenty-four of them. Plus it's not listed on his FD's, appears nowhere on his tax returns, and the phone's in the name of someone called Mulready . . ."

"Do you have an address?" Stuarti interrupted.

"Of course," Hobbes said, his tone hurt. "Skiff Mountain Road, outside a village called Kent. No number, just an RFD route, all mail to a Casey Realty."

"How's your memory?" Stuarti asked.

"Excellent," Hobbes said stiffly. "That's my . . ."

"Then remember *this*," Stuarti said. "This inquiry was never made, and you've never heard the name Matthews. Forget, and God himself won't be able to help you. You've got my promise on that."

"Anything wrong, sir?" his Mormon asked as Stuarti hung up the phone.

"Put on a tie," Stuarti said, "and get the car. I want to talk to a guy uptown."

When Kate had first met Matthews he had had another name. When she had learned, in broadest outline, what it was that he did, she came to suspect the name was false, and had challenged him. Cheerfully confirming her suspicion, he had nonetheless observed that it would perhaps be safest if she continued to know him only in his notional identity, and had suggested, with a diffident courtesy that had reassured rather than offended her, that she not inquire overmuch into his other life.

At first this had been an easy discipline, breached only in insignificant matters. Once, as the consciousness of a growing passion forced them to speak only of virtue, it transpired in a discussion of education that both of their mothers had been teachers of Latin, a vocation more taxing than normally thought, perhaps, since both were also dead. Another time, throwing ground rules to the wind after days of agonized indecision, she had asked him point-blank if he were married, to which he had responded gravely that he was not, and had never been.

Only later, in the days before he disappeared, had Kate, sensing somehow that an end of sorts was near and desperate to have something of him to keep, asked him how it was that he had come to do what he did.

His answer had been very brief.

"It was 1969," he had finally responded, "and the country was in the middle of a suicide attempt. It seemed," he had said, "an exaggerated response to ill-advised short-term policies."

Answering, Kate later realized, a question different from, though similar to, the one she had asked.

As she drove that afternoon from the school to her cottage, therefore, Matthews seated beside her in clenched silence, Kate was vividly conscious of her own helplessness. Knowing neither what sustained him, nor by what he was wounded (for Matthews, she somehow knew, was no more capable than the baby rabbit of articulating the nature of his injury), how could she heal him? Constrained by a precedent promise from which he had not freed and could not free her, Kate asked no questions.

Neither did she stop talking for an instant.

Spying a barn swallow on a fence post, she talked of birds.

Did the leaves not seem already to be turning? They did, and she rattled on unquenchably about carotene and cold nights.

As she spoke, she kept her hand on him always, touching his shoulder, his leg, his hand, and by the time they reached the cottage the sound of a human voice and the touch of a human hand had worked their therapeutic wonders sufficiently to free him from the terrible immobility that had held him.

Declining her suggestion that he try to sleep (in fear, Kate guessed, of dreams), Matthews accompanied her to the garden, sipping occasionally from the glass of ice and vodka that she brought him and gravely watching her pinch the sucker shoots from the tomato plants, as Kate shared with him all that she knew of aphids and slugs.

Driven inside at dusk by gnats, they sat quietly together in the kitchen, Kate polishing her mother's silver candlesticks as the room filled with the smell of heating ratatouille, speaking to him of her children, of their sadness and of their gaiety, of their small iniquities and their boundless kindness. Like most men, Kate noticed, Matthews seemed calmed by the sight of a woman working, and when she had finished the candlesticks, her only domestic silver, she continued with the flatware, which was stainless steel.

While Matthews barely touched his plate at supper, Kate was a believer in the power of example and cleaned hers with gusto, though each bite threatened to choke her. Refusing his offer to help with the dishes, Kate pointed Matthews to the room's single armchair, and when at last she turned from the sink, still extolling the virtues of the potato print as a diversion for rainy afternoons, she saw that he was asleep in the chair.

Covering his legs with an afghan, a gesture she could not deny herself though the temperature was nearly seventy, Kate watched him quietly for a moment, then wrote a note saying "I am in the yard," which she left on the floor beside him.

The grass outside was wet with dew. Before her was the great vista of night, stretching away, and above her a new moon held the old one in its arms. In the velvet darkness of the country night, the stars burned brilliantly; mere gases and fire, Kate knew, but eloquence, too.

Drawn by the gentleness, the quiet strength, the simple concentrated maleness of him, Kate had assumed, before, that Matthews would care for her. The realization, now, that it was she who must care for him changed nothing of importance. That they somehow completed one another, each requiring the other in order to be whole, remained for Kate the simplest and most undeniable of truths.

154

Seated on a fieldstone in the gentle night air, listening to the soft crunching sound of deer cropping crab apples in the orchard beyond, Kate felt in herself, despite her fear for him, an odd contentment and a simple and abiding sense of wonder and respect before the unknown in a human lifetime.

Angel Rivera, perspiring heavily, emerged from the garage bay of the A and L Meat Company on 133rd Street west of Broadway pushing a large canvas laundry cart. The cart was heaped with the bones of newly dead animals: a tangle of mammoth shin bones streaked with bright red blood, severed hooves protruding at impossible angles, a ball and socket joint as large as a basketball gleaming white in the afternoon sun. A small dark man with graying hair, Rivera grunted as he ran the cart up a short metal ramp and emptied the contents into a rusted metal dumpster at the curb. The dumpster was already half filled, and as the new bones tumbled onto those more sun-ripened the flies and sweet blood stench rose up to him in a humming cloud.

Leaving the cart on the sidewalk, Rivera stepped into the shadow of the garage bay, leaned gratefully against the wall, and pulled a cigarette from the pocket of his ruined polo shirt. Struggling with damp matches, he never saw Stuarti's Mormon until he was standing directly before him, credentials in hand, quietly explaining that the FBI required a word with him.

The field office to which Rivera was led, brandishing his green card before him like a cross before vampires, turned out to be the back seat of a four-door Plymouth Fury. Rivera's prior experience with federal authorities had not been reassuring, and the absence of interior handles and the presence of Stuarti in his cape did little to palliate his nervousness. It was thus with considerable relief that he learned that the authorities wished only to question him once again in his capacity as a witness to the beating of Denis McGuigan. Yes, he admitted readily, he had seen it all, and had already told the police everything that he had seen. No, he had no idea why it had happened, but though McGuigan had only worked at A and L Meats for six months, he had made a name for himself as a bully, and his colleagues had not mourned his mauling overmuch. Would he be so good as to recount again what he had seen? Yes, happily. The enforcer had been a blond man, pale, with glasses, and like Stuarti's Mormon had appeared out of nowhere . . .

Enforcer? Stuarti enquired curiously.

Oh yes, Rivera assured them. Professional, and fast like one had never seen. One moment Big Red had been leaning against the dumpster, smoking, and thirty seconds later, with his face beaten flat and open fractures to the number six, he would not have looked out of place inside it. Not even the pistol that McGuigan had always carried had been able to help him, Rivera said with awe, the one shot that he had been able to fire while falling no more slowing the enforcer than a slingshot might a rhino . . .

Asking his Mormon to give them a moment of privacy, and waiting for the door to close behind him, Stuarti quietly asked Rivera to repeat himself, and then explained his offer. He had six pictures, he said, and Rivera had one guess. Picking the right face was worth five hundred dollars. He would not be asked to testify, ever. Spreading the pictures on the seat between them, Stuarti took a deep breath. Did Rivera see . . .

"Chess!" the man said, with no hesitation at all. "Heem!"

"Sorry the pictures didn't work out, boss," Stuarti's Mormon said as they returned to Thirteenth Street. "But at least we got a better description. Blond guy, glasses, real pale skin . . ."

"A dangerous city, Floyd," Stuarti sighed, nothing in his voice to indicate that his wallet was lighter, or his heart heavier, than it had been before. "Never can tell when some myopic albino's gonna' flip out and decide to punch your ticket.

156

Let's stop by Fugazy on the way back and arrange ourselves a limo. I've had it with the seats in this Plymouth."

It was the enforcer's utter silence, Rivera had added as he left the car, that had been the most chilling aspect of the incident, but it was Stuarti alone, as they crawled downtown through a haze of diesel air, who guessed correctly to himself that the blond attacker's wordlessness had in no way been an act of practiced intimidation, but rather an ad hoc tactic, not wholly successful, employed to forestall weeping.

Kate was not sure how long she had been sitting in the dark when she heard the rattle of the kettle on her cast-iron stove and, turning, saw that Matthews had put on the light inside. For a few moments longer she lingered, reluctant to leave the night, then rose and strolled back toward the cottage.

She was ten yards distant when she heard the sound of voices from inside, and assumed that Matthews had turned on the radio in the kitchen. As she approached, she realized that it was not voices that she had heard, but rather a single voice, a woman's, and as she drew nearer still, and the voice became distinct, she was suddenly stopped in her tracks with horror, for the soft obscene sounds that drifted to her through the mesh of the rear screen door, staining the night air, could not, in any possible world, be coming from a radio.

As Kate stood riveted, her fist pressed to her mouth, the soft and strangled cries, as though of someone screaming underwater, began to build in anguish as they faded in strength, culminating at last in a lucid and hopeless whisper that sounded to Kate like "Lookit, Grandma!", before jerking abruptly to a stop, leaving only the dead hissing of the tape.

Shakily opening the screen door and stepping inside, Kate found Matthews sitting at the kitchen table, staring at a small tape recorder hissing on the oilcloth before him.

Hearing her enter, Matthews reached out and depressed

the Stop button, leaving them together in a silence utterly untouched by the chorus of peepers outside.

"Oh, my God, Tom," Kate said, her voice not wholly in control. "What was that?"

For a moment it seemed as though Matthews had not heard her, but then his head rose slowly and his eyes met hers, and Kate's heart turned over anew at the terrible intensity of his gaze, an intensity turned somehow inward, and unseeing.

"It was a girl dying," he said. "I have to use your phone."

Seated, her shaking hands clamped between her knees, Kate watched Matthews dial.

"Stuarti," said Stuarti.

"How's Weinstein doing?" Matthews asked, his voice chillingly conversational.

"He found him," Stuarti said flatly. "He says there's no doubt at all. When you and Priscilla were window-shopping at Balducci's, our friend Andreas was inside, looking out. You were right. You were only separated by two feet and a pane of glass."

"Can you get someone to open the library at Langley at this hour?" Matthews asked.

"Of course," Stuarti said. "What for?"

"I want the past three years of the Cuban party newspaper GRANMA," Matthews said. "I want the microfilm flown up, not faxed."

For a long moment Stuarti did not reply. When he did so, his voice was hushed.

"Son of a *bitch*," he breathed. " 'Look at GRANMA,' not 'Lookit, grandma.' It has to be a picture. That's what the bastard showed Priscilla and the girl that planted the bomb that Weinstein said impressed them so. Damn, Minihan's right. I'm getting senile."

"Don't feel too bad," Matthews said. "It's a distracting tape. How long will it take for the microfilm to arrive?"

"They can fly it into Teterboro," Stuarti said. "With the drive in, maybe three hours, tops. Where are you now?"

"I'll be there in two hours," Matthews said, and hung up. In the room, the outdoor night sounds were distant.

Looking squarely at Kate, Matthews said, "I have to go."

"Why?" she asked dully.

"Because if I don't," Matthews said, tapping the recorder, "the man who killed this girl will kill again and then go free ..." he paused, "... whereas, if I do, it'll only be one more poor dumb bunny that justice clouts. It's my job, Kate."

"Let someone else do it," she said desperately. "Get another job."

"Who'd have me?" Matthews asked, attempting a smile that ended only in a baring of teeth.

"My kids," Kate shot back. "In a flash. Me, too. The rest's only money."

"The money's not really that good," Matthews said, no longer smiling.

"Then why do it?" Kate snapped, regretting the words before they were out of her mouth.

"Well," Matthews said slowly, as though selecting one factitious argument from a host of possible candidates, "in the *Discorsi*, Machiavelli suggests that the only secure foundation for republican liberty is the military resolve of the arms-bearing citizen-soldier. He speaks of that resolve as *virtu* ..."

"And only means masculine will," Kate retorted, wounded by his tone though she knew its mocking harshness was not meant for her, but for some moribund ideal of his own. "Let someone else be virtuous. It's *killing* you! Oh, Tom," she said, her voice racing tears, "don't go!"

"Too late," Matthews said softly, standing. "It's only me he'll come for."

"Then don't die," she said fiercely, as the tears caught up, "and don't go crazy."

159

For a long moment Matthews held her close, and when at last he spoke his voice was tender.

"You're a dandy, Caitlin O'Kearney," he said gently. "Most people just say, 'Have a nice day.'"

And then he was gone.

CHAPTER NINETEEN

BY eight-thirty in the morning, the atmosphere in the West Thirteenth Street townhouse was, as Bullard had proudly remarked on returning with the breakfast, that of a team locker room in the hours before the big game. In actual fact, it was a bit tighter than that, and had Stuarti not glumly apologized, in his absence, for Bullard's unquenchable propensity to boyishness at such moments, it is likely that the remark would have been greeted with rudeness.

Stuarti and Minihan sat on the couch at one end of the living room, a bank of telephones ranged on the low table before them, blinking red lights on each indicating open lines. Minihan smoked without speaking, and Stuarti scribbled desultorily on his clipboard, glancing up occasionally at the television screen on which, soundlessly, a grim-faced Mr. Rogers was stuffing lettuce into the head-hole of a recalcitrant box turtle's shell.

In the kitchen, Bullard and Stuarti's Mormon were transferring elegant *delicatessen* from the brimming shopping bag with which Bullard had just returned onto a large pewter salver, Bullard crossly faulting the Mormon for his inadequate sense of presentation.

At the far end of the room, his back to the others, Matthews sat silently before a microfilm reader, steadily and slowly advancing the frames. On the wall above the machine hung an enlarged and detailed map of the two blocks around East Sixth Street and Avenue C, on which were marked, in felt-tipped pens of bright colors, the prospective positions that the various vans, support teams, and paramedics would take once Matthews was inside.

Next to the map was taped a single eight-by-twelve photographic enlargement of a man's head and shoulders, taken through a plate glass window. The man's hair was straw-colored and fine, his features Saxon and coarse, and his left ear and cheek were obscured by a hanging provolone cheese.

Matthews had been at the machine for the past three hours, and though Bullard had twice offered to spell him, Matthews had twice declined, the second time curtly. No one took offense at his shortness, nor at the way he held himself somehow private and apart, for each knew to the heart, whether with relief or shame or awe, that the day ahead held possibilities for Matthews that it did not hold for them.

Abandoning hope that the turtle would attack Mr. Rogers, Stuarti turned to Minihan.

"Where's Bunny now?" he asked.

Though Stuarti had last asked the same question five minutes before, Minihan said nothing, reached over, lifted a receiver, and murmured the word "Base."

Minihan listened for a moment and replaced the receiver.

"Still in traffic on the Grand Central Parkway," he said. "Looks like it's going to be the nine-thirty shuttle."

"What about your surveillance team at the G.M. Building?" Stuarti asked.

"Nothing so far," Minihan said patiently. "They'll go on checking in every half-hour 'til noon, though, same as they've been doing. If that's where Spats works, and we've got no guarantee of that at all, the next hour should be our best bet. Blaine tell you about the Porters?"

"He mentioned that there'd been some sort of nightmarish fuck-up," Stuarti said, "but we were talking about other stuff, and I didn't get the details. What happened?"

"It was awful," Minihan said. "Apparently both of them were a little slow bouncing back after Butterfield got his head splattered all over their library. Mrs. Porter complained that she kept on seeing his smile fly by every time she tried to sleep. Part of the problem, I guess, is that we couldn't tell 'em that the manifesto that the papers got was bullshit, and so they figured that there were still some lunatics out there who wanted to kill them. Made 'em real nervous. So, we put a guy on the house, and gave them an open line, hoped they'd feel a little better. Didn't work. Poor Mrs. P.'s calling about every half hour to report suspicious cars, which turned out to be *all* cars. They finally coked her to the gills on Thorazine, and that still only got it down to about every forty-five minutes . . ."

"Maybe someone should tell them," Stuarti said.

"Too late now," Minihan said, shaking his head. "So, the doctor decides Mrs. P. needs a little vacation, a change of scene. Turns out the Porters've got this summer place up in the Adirondacks, Tupper Lake. Just the ticket, the doctor says. Fresh air, lots of trees, no cars, so up they go . . ."

Here one of the phones on the table before them purred, and Minihan paused. He picked up the receiver, listened for a moment, and without speaking replaced it.

"Berg," he said. "She just left her apartment for the office."

"Right on time," Stuarti said, looking at his watch.

"They'll take her all the way," Minihan said, "and let us know when she's in."

"Good," Stuarti said.

"So," Minihan continued, "they get up in the country, Mrs. P. begins to relax a little, and one bright day Porter suggests that they have a picnic lunch. Why not? Mrs. P. hasn't been outside in a month, seems like a good idea . . ."

"Was it?" Stuarti asked.

163

"Nope," Minihan said. "They walk about a mile from the house, find a nice little clearing, and spread out their blanket. Mrs. P.'s killing ants and Mr. P.'s tryin' to get the Grey Poupon open when all of a sudden, WHAMMY!, about ten guys with huge pistols jump out of the woods yelling stuff like 'Gotcha, you motherfuckin' dinks! Freeze or die!' "

"Jesus!" Stuarti exclaimed.

"The guys're all dressed in military camouflage fatigues," Minihan said, "plus all of 'em are wearing these huge black goggles. Porter said it was horrible. They looked like Martians, or some kind of giant armed ants. Mrs. P. wasn't ready for it at *all*, and started going off like a siren. 'Gag that slope bitch!' the leader says, and so they gag Mrs. P. and tie them both up. 'All right,' the leader says, 'I'm only gonna ask you once. Where is it, and how many people are guarding it?' "

" 'Slope bitch?' " repeated Stuarti, aghast.

"Porter said it puzzled him, too," Minihan said, "what with Mrs. P. wearing about three hundred dollars' worth of picnic threads from Outdoor Traders, but just then he figured he had a bigger problem than someone callin' Mrs. P. names. 'Where's what?' he moans. 'Don't get cute with me,' snarls the guy. 'Where's your fuckin' flag?' 'We didn't bring a flag,' says Porter. 'That's it,' snaps the guy, and then he turns to the other Martians and says, 'Waste 'em!' "

"Holy shit!"

"Coupla guys step out, cock these huge pistols, and KA-VLAM! KA-VLAM!, suddenly Mr. and Mrs. P. both have these big white paint stains on their chests. Then the head Martian cuts them loose and gets all friendly. 'Sorry we had to kill you right at the beginning of the weekend,' he says, 'but it's a three-day game, and we figured we had to set an example. You folks need a ride back?' "

"*What!?*"

"Turns out it's a bunch of grown-up lunatics playing something they call the Survival Game. It's like Capture the Flag.

164

The head Martian was a dentist from Mamaroneck, and felt real bad when he found out they'd made a mistake . . ."

"No!"

"Yup," said Minihan. "I think maybe there're more loonies out there than the mental health people figure."

"How's Mrs. Porter?" Stuarti asked.

"Same question the director asked," Minihan said, "considering we were supposed to be taking care of them and everything. I talked to the psychiatrist who's treating her. Nice guy. First shrink I ever talked to that I could understand. 'I don't want to say that Mrs. Porter's around the bend,' he said, 'but from where I am I can't see her any more.' They've got her in Payne-Whitney, but they say it might be a while . . ."

"Ta-dah!" Bullard sang, as he marched out of the kitchen bearing the loaded salver. "Breakfast, everyone! We've got bagels, lox, cream cheese . . ."

The phone purred again and Minihan picked it up.

". . . kippers, melon balls, croissants . . ."

"Berg's in," Minihan said, replacing the phone.

". . . Westphalian ham, cress sandwiches, fresh orange juice . . ."

"For Christ's sake, Bullard," Stuarti snapped. "Get a grip on yourself! You sound like Mr. Mole rhapsodizing over Rattie's picnic hamper!"

"Drink this," Bullard said sternly, pressing a glass of orange juice on Stuarti. "Fresh vitamin C, pure health in a glass . . ."

A phone sounded again, and again Minihan responded.

"What?" he asked, after listening for a moment. "Is that right? Did you get a name? . . . Listen, Manny, you've done a good job. . . . No, stay right on him. If he starts to move at all, get back to me."

Minihan hung up.

"Bingo," he said softly into the waiting silence. "They

165

made Spats. He's the assistant director of the KAMA Purchasing Commission, a Soviet trade agency with offices on the thirty-seventh floor of the G.M. Building. Tenant information gives his name as a Korolev, Yuri . . ." Minihan's voice began to rise despite himself. "Bunny, Andreas, Berg, and Korolev," he said, counting on his fingers. "It's the four-link network you predicted, Ed, and no diplomatic immunity anywhere in sight. Jesus Christ! One agent serviced by three illegals! Baby-sitting Bunny must be all that the residency's N section is doing this season!"

The tension in the room momentarily dissolved into laughter and soft clapping, Bullard unsuccessfully attempting to propose a toast as Stuarti's whooping Mormon pounded him on the back. It was only after a few moments, therefore, that the general euphoria died, and the others, remarking Stuarti's face, followed his gaze to Matthews's back and noticed, for the first time, that Matthews, his hands by his sides, was no longer advancing the microfilm reader.

"Tom?" Stuarti said quietly.

For a moment Matthews did not respond, then he slowly stood and turned to them, his face expressionless.

"Our boy takes a nice picture," he said, almost to himself.

Proprietarily shouldering the Mormon aside, Bullard helped Stuarti into his wheelchair and pushed him across the room to the microfilm reader, the others following.

On the viewer was displayed the front page of the Cuban party newspaper GRANMA for May 18, 1984. The center of the page was dominated by a four-column photo, beneath which a caption read:

Hijos Valientes de la Revolución
Ayudad a los Defensores de la Libertad
En Tado el Mundo

The photo was a group of perhaps twenty young men in combat fatigues, mostly black. Some stood, some knelt; all held Kalashnikovs, and all regarded the camera with proud and self-conscious sternness. Behind the ranked trainees stood several Cuban soldiers in partial uniform, smiling paternalistically over the heads of their charges, and to the right, standing diffidently to one side, was a single European in civilian clothes.

His blond hair was fine, his features coarse, and he was, unmistakably, the same man who regarded them from behind the provolone in the larger photo on the wall.

"The Karlovy Vary camp in Czechoslovakia, would be my guess," Matthews said into the stillness. "That's HVA-run with Cuban trainers. Not that it makes much difference."

"This picture is priceless, Tom," Stuarti said in a hushed voice. "You know that, don't you?"

"Not without the guy that owns the face," Matthews said.

Stuarti's Mormon returned from the bedroom carrying Matthews's battered gym bag.

"Wireless transmitter," he said. "It's sewn into the handle mounting. It can't be felt. Only problem you might have is if he decides to take the bag apart."

Matthews took the bag with a curt nod of acknowledgment. Crouching to the floor by his chair, he replaced the athletic socks, sweat pants, jock strap, and handgun that were his baggage, and for a moment it was difficult for everyone not to reflect, given the journey on which he was embarking, that he was traveling very light indeed.

"Why not just seal off the whole block?" Bullard demanded nervously. "Or empty the goddamned building and fill it with our guys? That way once he's inside the perimeter . . ."

"Because we don't know that he'll even come," Matthews said, without looking up. "He may send someone else to test the water. Perhaps she's to call him. Or he calls her and if everything's right she picks up after the ninth ring. Or, for all we know, he lives in the apartment next door . . ."

"He doesn't," Minihan said. "Bullard reminded us to check."

"I want time," Matthews said, straightening and speaking only to Stuarti. "Even once you know he's inside, I want time."

For a moment Stuarti looked at Matthews without responding. As he did so, he noticed that one of Matthews's thumbs was bleeding, the skin at the base of the nail worried deep into the quick. When at last Stuarti spoke his voice was soft.

"You're going to try to talk him in, aren't you?"

Shrugging, Matthews reached for his windbreaker.

"Talk him in?" Bullard exclaimed. "Now that we've got that picture we simply don't need him alive! He's already murdered two people. For Christ's sake, Tom! The prospect of killing a man must be dreadful, but it would be suicide to try to . . ."

"Hush, Bullard," Stuarti said gently, and turned again to Matthews. Though it was clear that Matthews wished not to speak, Stuarti had no choice.

"Tom?" he repeated.

Slowly Matthews lifted his eyes until they met Stuarti's.

"Do you remember Barcikowski?" he asked softly.

"Yes," Stuarti said, his heart sinking an octave.

The words came in a tortured rush.

"On the day that he was shot," Matthews said, looking only at Stuarti and clearly oblivious to the sound of his own voice, "Barcikowski didn't know that he was going to die. His wife said later that he was concerned that he was catching a cold. He even had tickets to the Spartak game that weekend. But when he walked into the men's room at the Przemyśl station to clear a drop that afternoon, somebody was there already, waiting for him, and shot him in the face. In my dreams I've always imagined the shooter as a fat man, sitting on the toilet, perhaps . . ."

"Tom . . ." Stuarti said.

"Not *really* fat," Matthews continued with dreadful earnestness, "but sloppy, the sort of man who doesn't take care

168

of himself. In my dreams, so far, the shooter's face has always been in shadow. Then he begins to turn, and I wake up. The thing is, is that I have the dream a lot, and I'm not sure I could stand it if one day he turned before I could wake up, and his face was mine . . ."

Matthews's voice trailed away into silence. His eyes were unseeing and his lip beaded with sweat, and the effort of will with which he returned to himself pierced Stuarti to the heart to watch.

"Don't scare him," Matthews said abruptly, as though he had not spoken before, and his voice was suddenly firm again. "I want him calm."

"You'll have all the room you need," Stuarti said gently, ignoring the pressure of Minihan's leg against his. "Call as soon as you hear from Priscilla. And don't forget that the gym phone could be dirty by now."

From the doorway, Matthews turned and looked at Stuarti steadily. For a long moment Stuarti simply returned the gaze, love, or only tears, perhaps, shining in his eyes.

"Mind how you go, dear boy," Stuarti said softly.

Minihan's voice was icy when he spoke.

"I mentioned before, didn't I," he said quietly to Stuarti, "that your ferret struck me as a little . . . taut?"

"His name is Matthews," Stuarti snapped. "And yes, you did."

"Well," Minihan said, undeterred, "I'm going to do it again. The guy's having bad dreams when he's awake, for Christ's sake!"

"He's an old agent runner, Frank, like me," Stuarti said. "After a while you start thinking of agents as dependents, Frank, kind of like kids, and when you see one playing in the traffic you tend to get upset, no matter whose it is . . ."

"That guy is holding himself together with spit and baling wire, Ed," Minihan said flatly, "and he doesn't look like he can do it much longer."

169

"He won't have to," Stuarti said, so softly that Minihan could barely hear him. "Do you think the Bureau's got a friend in the Connecticut State Police?"

"I imagine so," Minihan sighed. "We're a friendly agency."

One of the phones on the coffee table sounded, and Minihan answered. Replacing the receiver, he turned to Stuarti.

"Bunny made the nine-thirty shuttle," he said. "He's on the way."

Stuarti breathed deeply, and looked squarely at Minihan as he spoke.

"You ever think about working for the Agency, Frank?" he asked.

"Sure," Minihan said. "Thirty years ago, same's you. I decided against it."

"The offer's still open, Frank," Stuarti said.

"Oh, Jesus," said Minihan.

"I mean if Bunny should accidentally get lost or anything," Stuarti said, "and the director turns out to be inconsolable."

"If Bunny gets lost," Minihan said, "I'm not the only one who's going to need an excuse, your nifty employment of the irresponsible passive notwithstanding, and I've never known you to be without one. I think I'll use yours."

"How's your hearing, Frank?" Stuarti asked.

"Excellent," Minihan replied shortly.

"The thing is," Stuarti said, "is that I've got to make a call to Washington now that you might want to say you didn't know anything about, later."

"Then I'll lie," Minihan said. "I don't even blush anymore since I've been taking the Inderal."

"I like a man who acts his age, Frank," Stuarti said fondly.

The line to Washington was open, and a voice responded as soon as Stuarti lifted the receiver and pressed a button.

"Let me talk to Irving," Stuarti said. "Irving? Listen, I've decided about the papers. It looks like today's going to be his first and last meeting, and I don't think we can count on him to grab everything we want him to have. Let's give him

the briefing papers for transmittal to the New York office. . . .
That's right . . . have you got the list? . . . Well, maybe *you*
don't, but I do, and you will too when you're my age. Just
get it." Stuarti sighed, waiting and doodling on his clipboard.
"Good, let me read them to you from mine. One, the agenda,
original copy. Two, the draft National Security Decision Directive, Xeroxed. Three, the technical abstracts, originals. And
four, the twenty-four-month testing schedule, Xeroxed. Right?
Good. . . . Nope, pad it out with anything you like. Those're
the four I'm concerned about. Let me talk to Eliot."

Stuarti hummed tunelessly, waiting.

"Eliot? Everybody ready? Well, this's your official call.
He's on the nine-thirty shuttle. It's a go. Load the Bunny . . .
yeah, me, too, only it feels more like dead moles in there than
butterflies. What? . . . Oh, right, you, too. . . . See you in New
York. . . ."

Stuarti hung up, shaking his head.

"I'm in a wheelchair and he tells me to break a leg," Stuarti
sighed. "Stay away from the theater, Frank, it'll rot your
brain."

"Load the Bunny?" Minihan moaned.

"Course TV's a different story, Frank," Stuarti continued
with inexorable brightness. "You don't even have to *have* a
brain. We've got ninety minutes here. Want to watch a little
'Begging for Dollars'?"

"What channel?" said Minihan finally, and it was only
when he stood and saw Bullard alone in the kitchen that he
noticed that Stuarti's Mormon was gone.

The call from Matthews came at 11:15.

No, Stuarti sighed grumpily, the feckless Darlene had yet
to check in from the previous night's revels, but should Matthews wish to leave a message he would add it to the others.

Matthews did.

"*Yeah*, I got it," Stuarti said crossly. "Call Norris at the
gym until five-thirty. You got a business appointment at six,

171

and won't be there after. Maybe one of you cheap bastards should think about buying her an answering machine, save all of us a lotta trouble."

Hanging up, Stuarti turned to Minihan.

"Matthews's going to Priscilla's at six," he said. "She must have called at eleven on the button. They aren't wasting any time."

"You think Andreas'll show?" Minihan asked.

"I agree with Matthews," Stuarti said. "The guy needs Weinstein and Priscilla dead yesterday, plus now he has to worry that Weinstein might get himself busted any minute and end up out of reach for good. They've already taken Matthews through one dry run, and he came up clean, and Matthews is the only one who can tell Andreas where Weinstein is. Yeah, he'll show."

"Time to decide about Korolev and Berg, then," Minihan said.

"Let's grab 'em," said Stuarti.

CHAPTER TWENTY

YURI Nikolaiovitch Korolev, carrying a large brief-case and sporting a burgundy wool suit, yellow socks, and tan East German shoes with heavily perforated toecaps, emerged from the Fifth Avenue entrance of the General Motors Building shortly after noon.

The day was rich with new spring warmth, the sky above a lambent blue, and the public scowl into which his heavy features composed themselves was more probably the *pro forma* expression of Soviet officialdom than a reflection of his mood, which, lunch looming, was one of contented anticipation.

Crossing Fifth Avenue, its traffic stream clotted with taxis and wealth, Korolev strolled through the Grand Army Plaza in front of the Plaza Hotel, where the rim of the fountain was rapidly filling with office workers carrying brown bag lunches and foil tanning reflectors.

Passing the fountain, and trailing in his wake a small army of FBI agents, Korolev continued leisurely to the Saint-Gaudens equestrian statue of William Tecumseh Sherman. The good general sat erect on his steed, Peace, with an olive branch in one hand and the horse's bridle in the other, leading him in hagiography as she had signally failed to do in life.

Untroubled by historical anomaly (a capacity, Stuarti sourly remarked to Minihan as they watched from the rear of a stretch limo parked across the street, of considerable utility to a Marxist functionary), Korolev stopped beneath the statue, and spreading a handkerchief to protect his dreadful suit from pigeon droppings, seated himself on the steps of the base. Opening his briefcase (which later inspection would reveal contained only a Reuben sandwich, a bottle of Dr. Brown's celery tonic, and the most recent month's copy of *Penthouse*), Korolev removed half of the sandwich, daintily arranged a napkin on his lap, and leaned happily back.

To his right sat an attractive secretary, her shoes in her lap and her nose in *Modern Screen* magazine; to his left a laborer in a sleeveless undershirt, his lunch pail on his knees and a preprandial sixteen-ounce Schlitz in his fist. Before him the pedestrian parade passed in review; messengers, madmen, suburban shoppers, and, stunning even at a distance in a yellow cotton sundress stopping well above the knee, Agent Barbara O'Casey of the FBI.

Hips swinging, eyes firmly forward in rejection of all invitations, Agent O'Casey approached carrying a cardboard tray from a local delicatessen, walking rapidly. As she passed the statue, however, the cynosure of all eyes and remarks, she appeared to catch a heel and stumble, dumping six ham-on-ryes and two tuna salad sandwiches to the ground. Visibly flustered, she bent to retrieve them, and as she did so a brisk following breeze, God's gift to the vigilant, lifted her short skirt entirely above her hips, exposing to view a spectacular bottom sheathed only in gossamer panties.

After a moment of awed silence, the steps erupted in cheers and applause, in all, such a merry din that the soft coughing sound from the lunch box of the laborer seated to Korolev's left was inaudible, even to Korolev himself. With a low grunt of agony, Korolev clutched at his chest and slowly and soundlessly toppled forward, eyes widening.

The symptoms that Korolev displayed—severe pain in the upper left quadrant of the chest, paleness and clamminess of the skin, and a shortness of breath so acute as to preclude speech altogether—were, bystanders later agreed, classically those of acute myocardial infarction. As such it must also have been dispatched, for barely had he hit the ground, it seemed, before he was surrounded by EMS paramedics monitoring his vital signs and administering oxygen (or *some* gas from a D cylinder) as they loaded him rapidly onto a gurney and into a waiting ambulance.

Afterward, one bystander actually claimed to have seen the EMS personnel approaching from Fifty-ninth Street *prior* to Korolev's attack, but it was generally agreed that in such moments of crisis sequence is often elusive. Another noticed, on the ground beneath Korolev's body when it was lifted, what seemed a tube of clear plastic two inches in length (and, had anyone bothered to measure, precisely nine millimeters in diameter) and hypothesized drugs as an explanation, but on examination the piece of plastic proved solid, and was dismissed as junk jewelry.

In all, as the ambulance sped away to the east and turned south on Second Avenue before extinguishing its lights and siren, it took less than ninety seconds to pluck Yuri Korolev unobtrusively and forever from one of Manhattan's busiest corners, and inconvenienced only Korolev himself, the plastic bullet causing two broken ribs and some inconsequential intercostal bleeding, and Cardiac Creases O'Casey, as the unfortunate agent in question came inevitably thereafter to be known in the Bureau.

"One down," Stuarti said to Minihan, peering at himself in the backseat vanity mirror and adjusting the knot of his unfamiliar necktie. "How do I look?"

"Like a banker," Minihan said.

"No need to be ugly about it, Frank," Stuarti said stiffly. "You could just say, 'Good.' "

"Good," said Minihan, and as he tapped the driver's window the limo slid gently into the midday traffic, heading for Rockefeller Center.

It was 4:46 when Mary Berg emerged, as was her habit, from the Fifth Avenue entrance of Rockefeller Center onto the sidewalk by the offices of Deak-Perera.

It was 4:47 when, having been briskly shown their credentials, she was led by two agents of the FBI to the rear door of Stuarti's limousine.

"Hi, Mary," Stuarti said, opening the door and peering up brightly like a chipmunk from its burrow. "Hop in."

Though her face was leached of color, her voice, when she spoke, was admirably composed.

"I am a citizen of the United Kingdom . . ." she began.

"And properly proud of it, too, I'm sure," Stuarti said, scooting over on the seat. "Get in."

Smoothing her skirt over her knees as the door closed behind her, Mary Berg looked around the interior of the limo, at the elaborate communications equipment lining the rear compartment, at the tape recorder on the seat between them, and at Minihan and the driver, seated behind glass in the front.

"You are also from the FBI?" she asked Stuarti.

"Nope," Stuarti said. "Those guys," he said, pointing to the two men standing silently outside the door, "are from the FBI. So're the guys in the cars behind us and in front of us. But I'm from somewhere else."

In the front seat with the driver Minihan softly spoke a single word that sounded suspiciously to Stuarti like "Mars."

"In what manner may I be of help to the FBI?" Mary Berg asked politely.

Stuarti sighed.

"In an ideal world," he said, "I suppose that you could

176

cut the crap, but I imagine that's asking a bit much after thirty years as an illegal. The problem is, Mary, is that we're a little short of time, here. Let's look at some pictures."

Opening a manila envelope, Stuarti removed six eight-by-ten prints. Wordlessly he handed the first one to her.

The photo was of her and Bunny standing together at the Central Park seal pond. The shopping bags at their feet were circled in red Pentel. When finally she spoke, Mary Berg's voice was tight.

"If he was indiscreet," she said, using Bunny's Christian name, "it was only because he cared about the future of mankind and believed in the work that we in the Campaign for Nuclear Disarmament are committed to . . ."

"Listening to the tapes of you and him together," Stuarti said, tapping the recorder between them, "and without wishing to seem unduly indelicate, the impression one gets is that his enduring commitments were to the future of mankind and your tits, and not necessarily in that order. As for being indiscreet, well, he was getting his little chain jerked by a pro, now, wasn't he? Let's just look at the pictures and save the narration."

Coloring, Mary Berg accepted the second photo.

It was of her and Yuri Korolev, deep in conversation on the sidewalk at the corner of Fifty-eighth and Fifth.

Mary Berg slumped in her seat.

The third photo, a Polaroid still smelling of processing fluids, was of Korolev, flat on his back on an ambulance gurney. His face was pallid, his eyes were dull, and an FBI shield was pinned to the sheet covering his chest like the tag on a trophy animal's ear.

"Yuri Nikolaiovitch is a little under the weather right now," Stuarti said, "but he should be fine for the trial. Unlike these folks."

The fourth photo was of Butterfield's headless body and the fifth showed the eviscerated corpse of the girl with the prominent nipples who had unwittingly planted the bomb.

177

Holding the photos, Mary Berg's hands began to tremble. That she did not weep, Stuarti decided, was an encouraging sign. She was, after all, English by training, and a business-woman; practical, competent, and by breeding and temper-ament of low annual tearfall.

The sixth and final photo, however, shook her badly.

The photo was of a narrow, two-bunk prison cell. Behind the bars stood an enormous black woman, at least six feet tall and with a musculature that suggested that anabolic steroids were as readily available in federal prisons as were more recreational drugs. Though the woman was smiling, her eyes were disturbingly wild, and the crude prison tattoo of a spider on her forehead compensated only marginally for the absence of her front teeth. Shirtless, she held a riding crop in her fist and sported an eighteen-inch dildo hanging obscenely from a leather belt around her waist.

"What's *that*?" Mary Berg gasped.

"That," Stuarti said proudly, "is Thelma-the-Roto-Rooter-Lady in her play clothes. Your new roomie up at Bedford Hills Correctional Facility. The staff'll be real glad to see you. Seems Thelma's been a little tough to manage since her last roommate died."

"She's *black*," exclaimed Mary Berg.

"And a bit self-conscious about it, too," Stuarti said. "Be gentle."

"My God!" whispered Mary Berg in horror.

"Choice time, Marya Dimitriovna," Stuarti said briskly, "and there're only two of them. Cooperate, or don't. Decline to cooperate, and you and Thelma live happily ever after. No trades, no Wolfgang Vogel, not even if they grab the presi-dent's wife. Cooperate, and after you spend a year or so in a nice comfy safe house getting debriefed, we provide you with a new identity and all of the opportunities that life in the West has to offer. Eat at McDonald's, get mugged, be unemployed, all the stuff they write about in *Komsomolskaya Pravda*. Up to you."

178

"You expect me to work for the CIA?" Mary Berg asked quietly.

"Why not?" Stuarti shrugged. "Marx once worked as a correspondent for the *New York Tribune*."

"What do you want me to do?" the woman asked leadenly, and though his face remained impassive Stuarti's heart erupted in hosannas.

"How good are your contacts in the Committee for Nuclear Disarmament?" Stuarti asked.

"Excellent," Mary Berg answered. "I'm a member of the steering committee."

"Trust you, do they?" Stuarti asked.

"Of course," she replied in a startled tone, no irony at all in her indignation.

"Then that's where we'll start," Stuarti said, and suddenly he was all business. "The CND has a rally scheduled for London's Hyde Park a week from this coming Sunday. I'd like you to contact several of your more radical colleagues on the steering committee. Explain, breathlessly, that you have been approached, in your capacity as a CND functionary, by a Very Senior Administration Official, who has come into possession of appalling documents pertaining to American nuclear strategy, and wants to do an Ellsberg. Make it clear that in the absence of an appropriate forum for his disclosures, both his information and his liberty are in imminent jeopardy. Perhaps they might have a suggestion."

"They will," Mary Berg said gloomily, in a tone that suggested that CND steering committee meetings had not always been an unqualified joy.

"Good," Stuarti said. "Now our boy returns from Washington on the shuttle sometime after seven this evening. On landing, he will be met by someone he's never seen before, who will give him a ticket on Air-India flight three-oh-two to London departing Kennedy at nine-forty P.M., and a message to call you immediately. Is there some word-code or anything that our guy should know about in order to identify himself?"

"Yes," Mary Berg said. "He should say, 'I am a friend of peace.' "

"Let's hope he can manage it without laughing," Stuarti said. "Now our boy's probably going to be a little nervous when he calls. He's got the crown jewels in his briefcase, after all, and somebody he's never seen before has just come up to him and sounded the big alarm. He's going to be in the market for advice and he'll call *you*. You're going to give it to him. You're going to tell him that the FBI questioned you today, about him. And that, among the other things, they wanted to know where he was today, and when he'd be back. Then you're going to tell him, as convincingly as you can, that his only chance now is to take whatever he's got and go public, fast, and hope that world opinion will see an agonized act of conscience, and reward him with its plaudits, where some humorless prosecutor might only see a violation of U.S. Code seven ninety-four, Section fifty-eight, sixty-one, and clap his ass into a federal prison for the rest of this century and as much of the next as it takes."

"Is there a script I'm supposed to follow?" Mary Berg asked bitterly.

"Certainly not," Stuarti said. "You've been managing him admirably for the past year, and I wouldn't presume to interfere. I want him to speak at the CND rally, Mary. How you make that happen's up to you. If he does what I want, dandy. If not, you and Thelma'll have plenty of time to figure out what you might have done differently."

Stuarti leaned across her, tapped on the rear window, and the door was opened.

"These gentlemen will take you home and stay with you," he said to the woman. "If I were you I'd try to get a little rest, Mary. We've got a busy week ahead, and lots of rehearsing to do. Good luck with the call. I'll be there around nine or so."

Visibly older than she had been fifteen minutes earlier, Mary Berg climbed woodenly from the limousine, accepting without protest the supporting hands that helped her from the car.

Above them, the bronze statue of Atlas stood on massive legs, the world on his shoulders and the Rockefellers at his back, haughtily ignoring the petty drama at his feet and St. Patrick's Cathedral across the street.

Stuarti rapped on the glass partition. "East Sixth Street, driver," he said, as Minihan slid the panel open, "and step on it."

" 'Thelma-the-Roto-Rooter-Lady'?" Minihan demanded.

"A Paris friend named Félicité who works the Porte St. Denis," Stuarti said as the limo swung away from the curb. "She's a staunch Gaullist and'll be pleased as punch to learn of her contribution to the geopolitical balance. Let's move."

CHAPTER TWENTY-ONE

IT was shortly after six when Matthews, strolling, rounded the corner into Sixth Street from Avenue B. The sun had already dipped behind the low buildings, and though the light endured the shadows were gently deepening to violet.

At the far end of the block, a municipal sanitation truck was completing its collections, the high straining whine of its compactor followed by an interval of low diesel panting as it gathered strength for its next bite. In its wake, battered metal garbage cans marked with their building numbers hung empty from thick chains, exhaling a fetid and carious sweetness.

The garbage truck, moving at civil servant pace, blocked the narrow street entirely, legitimating the cars that idled impatiently behind with their various and negligible human baggage. Across the street from Priscilla No-Last-Name's building a group of men, mostly Hispanic, stood drinking beer from paper bags, watching one of their number adjusting the carburetor of a crimson Chevy with dragon and flame decals. Though none paid Matthews the least attention, he noticed that their hair was, to a man, slightly shorter than one might normally have expected of a group of sidewalk mechanics.

On the corner by the bodega, a small knot of Hasidim stood locked in animated conversation, busy as geese. All wore beaver hats and voluminous overcoats against any possible chill, and the absence of side locks was not a detail an East German would be likely to remark.

Once, in preparation for a single meeting, Matthews had spent six weeks living in a small hotel in Belgrade's *stari grad*; coming to know the block—its cars, its faces, its patterns of commercial and pedestrian traffic—with the intimacy with which a proud homeowner knows his own back yard, until the slightest anomaly would have leaped to his eye like a neon sign.

Andreas would enjoy no such advantage.

All this Matthews saw as through a pane of thick glass, with a dreamlike clarity somehow muffled, distant, faintly distorted. In a single windowbox crocuses bloomed vividly, an unambiguous reality seeming briefly to admit the possibility that all truth need not be punishment.

Turning from the street—open, to his vision, like a drawer of knives—Matthews insouciantly entered Priscilla's building, an odd and buoyant joyousness, utterly unrecommended by circumstance, swelling in his breast. As he did so, a forgotten scrap of verse came to him, unbidden:

> *. . . like a child*
> *Who comes on a scene*
> *Of adult reconciling*
> *And can understand nothing*
> *But the unusual laughter*
> *And starts to be happy . . .*

Overhead what might have been an airplane passed, screaming with great power at a terrible height.

"Hurry up, for Christ's sake," Stuarti snarled at the driver as the limo slowed slightly in the traffic around Union Square.

"Take it easy, Ed," Minihan said. "We've got some forty people in place."

"Not inside the apartment, you don't," Stuarti replied grimly.

"We'll be there in three minutes," Minihan said soothingly, "and besides, there's nothing more you can do . . ."

Though intended as comfort, the words were no sooner spoken than Minihan regretted them, for when he turned to the back seat to speak again Stuarti's wrinkled face was tremulous with helpless anguish, the fear written as clearly as on a child's.

Unobtrusive in a knot of people surrounding a Sabrett's cart on the corner of Avenue B and Fifth Street, the East German accepted a wurst from the vendor, his smile like the dressing over a wound, as he watched Matthews enter Sixth Street from the north. On a stoop nearby, a fat young Puerto Rican woman had slapped her toddler, a little girl of three or four, and was screaming grim predictions for the child's future, as though by way of explanation for the blow. On the step above, her affectless young husband sat, a radio the size of a suitcase pressed to his head. The evening air was foul, heavy with the odor of stale cooking and bad digestion.

Crossing the littered street, the East German dropped the wurst onto an overflowing wire refuse basket—for his training had emphasized that such sidewalk food was as dangerous as subways—and began, slowly, to close on Matthews from behind.

That he felt no sense of danger, no reciprocal threat, was due, perhaps, to a subliminal conviction that no healthy man would ever hunt in this decay; that in this world of swarming, ratlike fauna the beauty of the predator was his alone.

By the time Matthews entered Priscilla's building, the East German was less than fifty yards behind him.

"Willkommen!" smiled Priscilla brightly, exhausting her newly acquired knowledge of German as she held the door wide for Matthews. "C'mon in, Jack. You want a drink, or do you just want to play?"

"A drink," Matthews said, entering.

The room was empty, the bathroom door ajar.

"Help yourself," Priscilla said, her voice a hair tight. Behind him, the bar of the police lock rattled twice. Locked, then opened again.

Matthews poured himself a Cognac from the bottle of Remy. Priscilla approached, smiling, her body between Matthews and the door.

"I assume you mean a drink *first*," she said, her hand touching the front of her body almost absently.

"How stoned are you?" Matthews asked.

"Oh, enough, I think," she said, the clenched smile unchanging on her face. "But if not, I can always fix it."

"Sit down," Matthews said.

The girl sat on the edge of the low couch, her eyes wary. As she watched, Matthews stripped to the waist, folding his windbreaker and shirt neatly and placing them on the table before him. Reaching into his gym bag, he then withdrew a pistol in a clamshell holster, from which he easily thumbed the clip, placing both on top of the clothes. His thick hand closed momentarily on the handle of the gym bag, and there was a faint cracking sound, as though of a delicate mechanism breaking.

"What are you doing?" the girl asked.

"You told your friend Andreas that I carry," Matthews said quietly. "Under the jacket, behind. I don't want to get shot by mistake."

"Andreas?" Priscilla asked, licking her lips and looking at Matthews with a swerving, underbrow glance.

"The guy you just left the door open for," Matthews said matter-of-factly. "The guy that blew off Walter Butterfield's head with a booby-trapped phone and gutted your friend Fran as a reward for helping. *That* Andreas."

"Some friend," Priscilla finally said sulkily, no human impulse that Matthews could understand in her face. "She tried to fuck him the first day she met him."

The sickening brutality of the girl's response seemed suddenly and somehow to open a door in Matthews's mind directly onto what seemed an inferno. A roaring filled his ears, and before his eyes a vast and smoking darkness yawned, lit spectrally with lurid flames and searchlights of great intensity, like an oil refinery at night.

Putting the vision from him with an effort of will, Matthews turned and faced the girl.

"How long do we have to wait?" he asked. Fighting a yawn, he was startled to find that he could not hear his own voice.

Neither could he understand the girl's answer, which was short, but when he followed her eyes to the door he noticed that it was opening, soundlessly, metal sliding on metal in impossible silence.

"Not long," she must have said.

They had watched him approaching down the block from the west, following in Matthews's steps, though with the light behind him it was only when the chunky blond man in the blue sports coat hesitated for an agonizing moment in front of Priscilla's building before entering that they clearly recognized his face as that of the man in the provolone photo.

"That's him," Minihan said to Stuarti, his breath coming more rapidly despite the tight rein on his voice. "That's Andreas." Leaning forward, he spoke into the hand radio connecting him with the surveillance teams assigned to the rear and roof of the building. "He's in! Repeat! He's in!"

In the back of the limo, a frantic Stuarti furiously punched his radio receiver twice before slumping back on the seat.

"Oh, goddamnit," he whispered, eyes wide. "Matthews has turned off his transmitter."

"He's going to kill the guy," Minihan said uneasily. "I can see where he might not want that on tape . . ."

"No," Stuarti said, almost to himself. "He's not."

"Give him time," Minihan said. "You promised to give him time . . ."

"Third floor, right?" Stuarti snapped.

"Yeah, third rear . . ."

"Ten seconds a floor," continued Stuarti, his voice gathering volume, "that's thirty seconds." He looked at his watch. "Time's up!" Leaning forward, Stuarti splayed his chubby fingers on the radio keys like an organist, depressing as many as he could. "Go! Go!" he shouted, *"Now!"*

"There's no voice link in close, Ed," Minihan said. "The street guys are using vibrating pagers . . ."

But by then Stuarti had the back window down and was screaming, *"Go, you dumb bastards!"* at a puzzled group of passing Hasidim, whose grim faces indicated that their critical estimation of the New World was only confirmed by the spectacle of an elderly millionaire screaming anti-Semitic abuse from the rear of his limousine.

The man in the blue sports jacket stood framed in the room's doorway, a heavy pistol steady in his fist, impassively regarding the half-naked Matthews and the holstered gun on the table before him. Though he was clearly the man in the photograph identified by Weinstein, the features beneath the flaxen hair were somehow thicker, more repellent, than they had been in the still photo. His eyes were narrow and colorless, and animated by a cunning, porcine intelligence.

"You are Mr. Norris?" he said softly, the accent every bit as thick as Weinstein had described it.

His feet up on the low coffee table and his hands folded carefully in his lap, Matthews replied, equally softly, in German.

187

"No," he said, "I am not. 'Norris' was simply a name I used, as you have used 'Andreas.' Listen to me. You are an agent of the Hauptverwaltung Aufklärung on loan to the KGB. Your principal in this country, now in custody, is Yuri Korolev of the KAMA Purchasing Commission. This building is surrounded by agents of the FBI. Nothing that you can do here can prevent your arrest. Do you understand what I have said?"

As Matthews spoke, the flaxen-haired man's face began to darken, blotching angrily as his features gathered into a frown. Above the narrow pig eyes the skin of his forehead tightened into hard red ridges, like the palate of a dog.

"So?" he snarled, his inadequate English betraying him into petulance. "So?"

"They've said they'll give me time," Matthews continued as evenly as he could. "They won't. They can't. Lie face down on the floor with your hands in sight. Slide the gun across the floor away from you. Do it now."

Though the blond man did not move, a faint expression of hesitation passed across his features like a shadow.

"*Please* listen to me," Matthews whispered, suddenly close to tears. "I know how alone you feel! But for God's sake, choose to live! Lie down! Be my friend! Perhaps there is the possibility of . . ."

Here Matthews's German failed him. Wanting the word "forgiveness," he could only think of "*verzeihung*," which meant "pardon," and was not at all the same thing.

Priscilla, however, listening to Matthews's German with the same appalled fascination she might have shown had he suddenly sprouted a second head, had advice of her own to offer.

"Kill him!" she screamed, gathering her feet beneath her and leaping from the couch.

Perhaps it was the sudden shattering of the silence, perhaps the unexpected motion; perhaps, even, given the man's English, a moment of confusion in regard to her predicate object.

188

At the sound, in any event, the man's legs flexed instantly into a shooting crouch, his left hand dropped automatically to brace the pistol, and with the sound of a thunderclap in the small room, he fired.

The bullet caught Priscilla on the rise, just above the lip. Her head exploded like a melon.

At the same moment, Stuarti's Mormon, firing a 12-gauge Ithaca pump gun from the doorway at the end of the hall, cut the East German very nearly in half. The shot load struck him in the spine, seeming for a moment to draw him backward before hurling him forward into the room, a piece of his chest wall the size of a bread plate preceding him.

Matthews sat on the couch, his legs still up, unmoving. In the sudden silence his humming seemed quite loud. He was aware of a sharp stinging sensation above his left eye, and of a deeper pain in his chest, making it difficult to breathe. Above all there was a desire for sleep. His glasses were speckled with blood and matter, and he removed them carefully, folding them on his lap. Doing so, he noticed with detached curiosity, failed to clear his vision. As he wiped his face, the blood pooled in his hand.

"*Vergebung*," he whispered, forgiveness coming, as it so often does, too late.

Amid a babble of rising voices, he gave himself to sleep.

Stuarti was in the entrance hall, squeezing past the Goya boxes, when the spasm of gunfire erupted. With a scream of frustration he hurled the forearm crutches from him, lunging for the banister, and would have fallen had not two FBI agents caught him. One pushing, one pulling, one cursing, the three of them clawed their way up the stairs as other agents and paramedics sprinted past.

The third floor hallway was filled with the stink of cordite and blood. Indistinct in the hanging smoke, Hasidim stood everywhere, bristling with automatic weapons like a vision from a JDL fantasy. Agents wearing jumpsuits and baseball caps descended the stairs from the roof, carrying long guns. Occasionally a radio crackled and spoke.

At the far end of the hall the door to Priscilla No-Last-Name's apartment stood ajar. Blood everywhere, the interior of the room looked like a slaughterhouse. Spattered with gore, Matthews lay on the floor beside the couch, one paramedic monitoring his blood pressure as another taped a compress dressing to his chest. Empty boxes of surgical gauze littered the floor. Other paramedics stood quietly by, the absence of a head or chest being generally accepted as diagnostic signs contraindicating attempts at life support.

Stuarti slumped to the landing, his vision swimming and his breath rasping in his chest. An acrid fluid filled his mouth, which he forced himself to swallow.

Unbidden, Stuarti's Mormon came and crouched beside him, placing a hand on Stuarti's shoulder.

"Matthews'll be all right," he said softly. "He had a pellet bounce off a rib. He's also got a cut over the left eye, but not from a pellet. A button or a piece of bone is what they guess. He'll be OK."

"Good," Stuarti said, swallowing another mouthful of bile.

"He had his coat and shirt off," the Mormon said, more softly, "and his gun was on the table, unloaded. I don't know what the hell he was thinking of."

Turning his head, Stuarti gazed into his Mormon's face, radiant with new confidence and murderous innocence.

"No," he said finally, "no, you don't. Good job, Floyd."

"Thanks, boss," said the Mormon, in a tone which, in another context, Stuarti might have described as one of deadly earnestness. "Where're your crutches?"

"I don't know," Stuarti said dully. "Downstairs, I think."

"Here," said Minihan quietly, holding them.

The Mormon pulled Stuarti to his feet and began to help him from the landing, until Minihan wordlessly shouldered him aside.

Together the two old men descended the stairs.

" 'Boss,' " Stuarti repeated softly, his voice distant.

"Pull your socks up," snapped Minihan, "and watch where you're going."

"Sorry, Frank," Stuarti said wanly. "I'm feeling a little old."

"You *are* old," Minihan said sharply. "So what? Want me to call the Home?"

"Ta mère," Stuarti said, his voice weak but his face grateful.

"Better," said Minihan. "Not good yet, but better."

In the lobby Stuarti managed to stand unaided, tucking in his shirt and straightening his tie. Failing to find a handkerchief, he bent and blew his nose on his fingers, shaking them clean and then drying them on a Goya box.

"Everything I've heard about the French is true," Minihan said, recoiling in disgust.

"Where's Bunny now?" Stuarti asked.

"On the Eastern shuttle," Minihan said. "He gets into LaGuardia at seven-fifteen."

"I understand he missed that one," Stuarti said. "That he won't get in until after eight."

"That's not what the guy said on the car phone," Minihan said.

"Crossed wires," Stuarti continued reassuringly. "Happens all the time. It'll give your guys at the gate time to grab a little coffee."

"You expect me to pull back the airport surveillance?" Minihan sighed.

"Not far, and not long," Stuarti said. "Five minutes ought to do it."

"Five minutes, tops," Minihan said seriously. "If the guy's going to fall through a crack it's going to have to be a small one, or some poor bastard ends up in Anchorage. With me."

"A small one'll be enough," Stuarti said, fitting himself into the forearm crutches.

"Don't forget they've got twenty-four-hour cameras in the

gate areas, Ed," Minihan said. "Anybody that talks to Bunny's likely to end up on film, and that's airport security. I can't touch it."

"Stay with Matthews, OK?" Stuarti said. "And make sure they keep him at St. Vincent's. If he looks restless, get the doctor to sedate him. I should be back by eight or so. Tell him I'll see him there."

Ignoring the stares of the uniformed patrolmen sealing off the building, Stuarti emerged into the darkening street, sticks stabbing the pavement before him. Approaching the limo, its driver with his shield stuck in the window, Stuarti saw two Connecticut state troopers standing by the rear doors. The nearest one snapped to attention as he approached.

"Mr. Stuarti, sir?" the trooper asked.

"That's me," Stuarti said wearily.

When the trooper opened the rear door, Stuarti bent and essayed a small bow, nearly falling into the car as he did so.

"Miss O'Kearney," he said. "Thank you for coming."

Kate's face was taut with anxiety, but her voice, when she spoke, was strong.

"It's about Tom Matthews, isn't it?" she said.

"Arthritis," Stuarti said apologetically, crawling into the back seat on all fours. "But when I was young I was a dancing fool."

"Is he dead?" Kate demanded. "Tell me now, please, if he is."

"No, he's not," answered Stuarti, patting her hand, then righting himself with difficulty on the seat, "and, yes, it is. LaGuardia Airport, driver. The shuttle terminal."

CHAPTER TWENTY-TWO

A T first Kate could only weep with relief, her shoulders shaking with her sobs. The rush hour was ending, and the shuttered shop fronts of lower Broadway slid rapidly and soundlessly past the smoked windows of the limousine as it sped downtown, its high beams flaring from time to time as it overtook slower vehicles. Stuarti sat beside her in the back seat—saying nothing, though he ached to stroke her hair—and it was only when they turned left into Chambers Street, the Municipal Building looming before them, that Kate's weeping finally slowed and spent itself, until all that was left was fear like a stone in her chest.

"Where is he?" she asked dully, as they swung around the Municipal Building and onto the Brooklyn Bridge, hanging facedown from its strings before them. "Where's Tom?"

"Please don't worry," Stuarti said gently, allowing himself to pat her hand. "He's all right. You'll be with him within the hour. But I need a few words with you first, Miss O'Kearney, and this is the only time we'll have."

"Who are you?" Kate demanded, blowing her nose.

"Just an old bag with a soiled name, dear," Stuarti said gently, "and gone in the withers to boot. But in my own way

I love Tom, too, dear girl, and wish him well. Please believe me."

"You're his old Paris friend, aren't you?" Kate asked. "The one he thinks so highly of."

"His *mature* Paris friend," Stuarti said. "And yes, I am."

Slowing, the limousine exited into Brooklyn Heights, doubled back beneath the bridge, and after passing through a dead zone of warehouses and empty sidewalks swung up an access ramp and onto the Brooklyn-Queens Expressway. Tenting his fingers, Stuarti began to speak.

"In the fifties," Stuarti said, "there was a popular joke, with endless variants, in which a housewife explains to a friend how the decisions are made in her marriage. 'I make all the unimportant decisions,' she says, 'and my husband makes all the important ones.' 'What's important and what's unimportant?' her friend asks. 'Well,' the housewife answers, 'I make all our budget decisions, I decide where we go on vacation, I decide on the children's schools . . .' 'Then what does your husband decide?' her friend asks. 'Oh,' the woman says, 'he decides what we should do about desegregation, the Middle East, Red China. . . .' " Stuarti smiled, distantly. "It was a 'private' time, you see, and involvement in anything other than one's 'private' concerns seemed not only pompous and futile, but ridiculous. People laughed."

To their right sprawled the desolation of Williamsburg. Here and there stood vacant buildings marked for demolition, with white X's on the windowpanes and the airshafts indicated as a safety courtesy to thieves.

"By 1970," Stuarti continued, "when I recruited Tom in Paris, that joke was not merely no longer funny, it was incomprehensible. The mood had changed, you see. The country was in convulsions, and the obligation to act seemed a clear duty. Sociologists have written that the domestic turmoil caused by Vietnam produced a generation characterized by cynicism and disillusionment. Now you are too young to have

194

been a child of that generation, and I too old to be a parent, but I don't believe that's right. Our children were much too strong, too *good*, for that. My experience suggests, instead, that we produced a generation of idealists and romantics, forced to the sort of decisions that life had not yet had the time to teach them how to make.

"There were many who, in the best of faith, perceived the United States to be the single major threat to peace and freedom. They burned their draft cards and took their broken hearts to Canada. Or went nuts. There were others who, with the simple good luck of a slightly larger historical perspective, saw this widespread perception itself as a grave threat *to* the United States, and thus to freedom's brightest hope. They did other things. Were you to ask Tom what he's been fighting for for sixteen years, and were he to answer you—which he would not, yet—I can easily imagine him looking you squarely in the eye and saying: 'For democracy. For the disestablishment of privilege and the right to a trial by jury. For the career open to talents, and for popular sovereignty expressed through representative institutions. For absolute freedom of speech and press, and for total religious toleration.' And it would be the *truth*."

Though Stuarti's voice was soft, his intensity redeemed his words from sententiousness and, like a rediscovery of love, gave new life to what otherwise would have been stale cliché.

"Tom was wonderful," Stuarti said simply. "He believed passionately in what he was doing, and instilled that passion in the people he worked with. Agents did things for him that they would have done for no one else, believing, correctly, that they were only acting as Tom himself would have acted in their place. . . ."

"Bless you," Kate said. "Are you trying to tell me that Tom's a fine man?"

"Yes," Stuarti said firmly. "I am."

"Why?" Kate asked. "I already love him."

"Sixteen years is a long time," Stuarti said, his voice distant as they passed over the Kosciusko Bridge, Manhattan twinkling off to their left.

"Yes?"

"Tom's tired," Stuarti said softly. "It's difficult to explain. It's less one's belief that erodes than one's capacity to cast things starkly, in blacks and whites. Ambiguity creeps in, and you find yourself fighting paralysis. Some drink, some weep at night, some find themselves getting a little too rough with others for their own good . . ."

"And some throw up," Kate advised him. "What are you trying to say?"

"It's time for Tom to quit," Stuarti said, his voice still quiet. "To join the real world, have a family, go on to the next thing . . ."

"Tell *him*," Kate breathed. "I don't require any convincing at all."

"I plan to," Stuarti said, turning to her. "But I'm afraid I need your help."

Kate looked at Stuarti for a long time before she spoke. About them was an infinity of single-family houses where, in interchangeable boxes of gingersnap brick set on contiguous quarter-acre plots, lives were being led, dinners eaten, the news watched.

"Shouldn't that be his decision to make?" Kate asked quietly.

Ahead an exit sign read Grand Central Parkway/LaGuardia Airport.

"In his memoirs," Stuarti said, "George Ball, speaking to the absence of a wife in Adlai Stevenson's life, bemoaned Stevenson's lack of what he called 'the institutionalized candid friend.' It seemed a nice definition of a wife."

"Meaning that I should make my own judgment," Kate said.

"If there were time for you and Tom to consult, I'd urge you to," Stuarti said, lying only a little. "But there's not.

Perhaps you could think of yourself as a candid friend out of wedlock."

When next Kate spoke, her voice was a bit shaky, but her resolve unmistakable.

"What do you want me to do?" she asked.

"To trust me," Stuarti said simply. "And to take a big risk."

"*After* that," Kate said impatiently, her voice already better.

"I want you to talk to a man at the shuttle terminal," Stuarti said, withdrawing an envelope from his briefcase. "To give him a message and an airline ticket. And to keep your best side to the security cameras at all times."

Before them the traffic on the Grand Central Parkway flowed in a liquid stream of light, the low cloud cover above the airport illumined luridly from beneath, as though by a great fire.

CHAPTER TWENTY-THREE

IT was eight-fifteen when Stuarti entered Matthews's room at St. Vincent's Hospital. Though he had not slept in more than twenty hours, his air, despite the crutches, was jaunty, and the lines of worry and fatigue that an hour before had etched his cheeks had been somehow brushed away, a faint smell of Dewar's suggesting more precisely how.

The room contained two beds. Matthews lay easily on that nearest the window, his legs covered with a sheet and his bare chest swathed in adhesive tape, drinking coffee as he patiently answered the questions of a nervous young intern. Minihan sat in a chair next to the bed, listening quietly.

No, Matthews had had neither scarlet fever nor whooping cough.

No, no family history of high blood pressure. None at all.

Following the telephone cord with his eyes as it pulled taut from the wall jack, passed beneath the empty bed, and snaked around the corner before disappearing into the bathroom, Stuarti, with a wave to Matthews and Minihan, pushed open the bathroom door to find Bullard seated on the toilet, drumming his fingers as he waited for yet another outside line.

Seeing Stuarti, Bullard replaced the receiver in the cradle and stood.

"Anything I need to know?" Stuarti asked quietly.

"Tom'll be fine," Bullard said. "One of our doctors is on the way, but the trauma guys here say no problem."

"Good," Stuarti said.

"The local cops, what with all the federal credentials, think it was some big drug thing. We're letting them think that for right now. Also Matthews was carrying the Norris ID, so that's how they've got him here. We didn't see any particular reason to set that one straight right away, either."

"Good."

"They've got Andreas John Doe'd at the Bellevue morgue. We'd got the pictures already, and so we decided to let the press go with the bodies, rather than bother us here. Midtown South wanted a statement from Floyd, but Frank axed that, told them to wait for the Bureau report . . ."

Stuarti put his hand on Bullard's shoulder. Bullard's face, too, was clawed with fatigue.

"When this thing started," Stuarti said, "I asked Blaine for an administrator who could keep the bureaucratic heat off us, take it himself if need be. I haven't felt any heat, and I'm not so dumb as to think that's because there wasn't any. You've done a good job, Bullard."

"There's something I'd like to say," Bullard said stiffly.

"Say it."

"A few weeks ago," Bullard said, "I referred to Tom as a thug. I was wrong."

"Go back to the apartment and get some rest," Stuarti said, gently patting him. "The next few days are going to be a little bumpy, bureaucratically, and we're going to need you at your best."

For a moment Bullard's eyes filled with gratitude, then squaring his shoulders into that posture natural to a needed man, he turned and strode away.

*   *   *

"How did it go?" Minihan asked, as the young intern left and Stuarti joined them.

"Disaster," Stuarti replied cheerfully. "The little devil got clean away, right under the noses of the FBI. No wonder you guys don't have your own TV show anymore."

"Which," Minihan sighed, rising, "means my red phone should be ringing off the hook right about now."

"Tell the director I said I'm sorry," Stuarti said. "Remind him that everyone makes mistakes. And keep Bunny's name off the goddamned Customs Service Watch List for another eight hours."

"Good luck, Tom," Minihan said, extending his hand to Matthews. "Take it easy."

"You, too," Matthews said, taking the hand and returning Minihan's gaze. "And thanks."

"Sure," Minihan said, and with a vague see-you-later wave to Stuarti he turned and left.

"Nice guy, Frank," Stuarti said with open curiosity, wondering what words had passed between them, but Matthews was not to be drawn and merely nodded his assent, his eyes on Stuarti. Matthews's left eye was already darkening with bruise; the bristling black sutures above had turned his eyebrow into a caterpillar.

"A doctor in Vienna once told me," Stuarti said, maneuvering himself onto the room's other bed and lifting his legs with his hands, "that what he called 'a life of wice' would kill me. He was wrong. Wice agrees with me just fine, but another eight hours in the back seat of a car might do it." Picking up the bed's control panel, Stuarti stabbed a button and moaned with pleasure as the bed whirred into a supporting position. "And you, dear boy? Here you are, *nel mezzo del cammin* and all that, with a nice new bullet hole. Given any further thought to a career change?"

A nurse entered with a collection tray of urine samples and glared at Stuarti sprawled on the made bed.

200

"None for us, thanks," Stuarti said brightly.

"It was only a pellet," Matthews said.

"Quick, nurse," Stuarti said. "It's made of lead and it comes out of the end of a gun, fast. What do you call it?"

"A bullet?"

"Thank you," Stuarti said with quiet dignity, dismissing the nurse with an airy wave and turning again to Matthews. "How about teaching languages?" he continued earnestly. "With your command of the idiom you'd be a whiz. 'Le truc de mon oncle est dans le machin de ma tante,' that sort of thing. Or perhaps tourist Russian? 'Yah vash grotesque police state loo-bloo . . .'"

"I didn't want the dreams," Matthews said quietly, in his voice a note of helpless wonder that briefly threatened to capsize Stuarti's carefully maintained composure.

"Of course, dear boy," Stuarti said, his voice thick. "You're tired."

"It's only partly that," Matthews said, still struggling toward an unattainable clarity. "You see, I have a friend . . ."

"I know," Stuarti said softly, conscious even as he spoke of the risk. "She and I just returned from the airport together."

Above the adhesive tape encasing his ribs, the muscles of Matthews's thick flat chest gathered, the lines beneath them drawn as crisply as with a fine-nibbed pen. His head turned slowly, and his eyes, when they found and held Stuarti's, were as flat and depthless as a snake's.

"What?" he whispered.

"Oh, Christ," Stuarti sighed. "Should I have brought my Marlin Perkins Thorazine dart gun, or are you gonna let me talk?"

"Go ahead," Matthews said, unblinking.

"I haven't told this story before," Stuarti said, reaching over and grabbing Matthews's ginger ale from his table, "but I can use the practice, since I'm going to have to tell it several times in the next few days, and if this isn't the final version it'll be near enough. You want this ginger ale?"

201

Matthews, apparently, did not.

"I call it the story of the Bunny and the Sackpig," Stuarti began, fluffing his pillows and settling back with his ginger ale in his fist. "Once upon a time, there was an ambitious featherhead of a systems analyst who decided that he wanted to be Daniel Ellsberg when he grew up. He was encouraged in this odd ambition by his new paramour, whom he believed to be an Englishwoman active in the Campaign for Nuclear Disarmament, and got himself a low-level job with the ACDA, but with access to high-level information. He didn't know what the hell he was grabbing, of course, but he grabbed it anyway, with the predictable result that INR security—happily headed by an old friend of ours—had his number in less than a year.

"The question then addressed by an extremely small group of people became what to *do* with the dumb son of a bitch. Prosecute him? The poor dummy's doing it for the glory, not for money, he doesn't know his new friend's a ringer, at least not at first, and if his motives are a blend of idealism and sex, well, whose aren't? A trial would be awful. Imagine putting the guy on the stand for a month and having him blubber about saving the world while some werewolf from Justice tears at his throat. It'd be like having Spiro Agnew beat up Pete Seeger on prime time. Was there not some way, the question was asked, to turn this small liability into a large asset? Time to call the Wizard."

"An overseas call, was it?" Matthews asked.

"Of course," Stuarti continued. "And despite advancing years and delicate health, the Wizard graciously agreed to cross the ocean, at great cost to his comfort and convenience, to explore the possibility of more fully exploiting this potential asset. To which end, the Wizard surrounded himself with a crack team of experts. Unknown to the Wizard, however, one of his experts, a security guy he'd worked with in Bloc Operations, had developed a loose screw. The Wizard was warned—it's on the record—but chose to ignore the warning, which was a mistake, for the guy with the loose screw began to Have Doubts.

"He suspected that the mark was a Willie—a suspicion that is also on the record—and thus the victim of a double con game. He also knew that society's acceptance of *any* con game depends partly on dehumanizing the victim, which he had lost the ability to do, and on being willing to ignore the implications of legitimating the con." Stuarti sipped delicately at his ginger ale. "*You* know, no ethical norm or public policy that takes account of the damage done to the agent, the victim, and society. Society as Iago, that sort of thing. I've got to work on it a little more, maybe run it past the Department of Nifty References, but that's the general idea . . ."

"And Kate?"

"It'll probably be about what you might imagine," Stuarti shrugged. "The guy with the loose screw had a girlfriend and they talked about it. Probably in more detail than was prudent. Finally she couldn't stand watching her lover go nuts. Decided that if tipping the Bunny off and letting him run for it was the price of the guy's sanity, then it was worth the cost. Something like that. The airport security photos ought to speak for themselves."

"She wouldn't do that," Matthews said.

"Of course she would," Stuarti said. "We're speaking of a woman of exceptional character, Tom. She'd do whatever she felt she had to in order to protect someone she loved. Wouldn't you?"

They regarded one another in silence.

"She knows?" Matthews asked.

"About the NORAID guys?" Stuarti said. "No, she doesn't. That's your business. Do you imagine that she would love you less?"

"I don't know," Matthews said, very quietly.

"Then perhaps you should tell her and find out," Stuarti said. "But as I said, that's your business. Now what I plan on telling *them* is this. Listen, boys, try to drag the girl into court, and the guy'll take the stand and tell classified stories that'd stand your hair on end. All of them true. Leave the girl alone, and let the guy retire quietly would be my advice—no exit bio, no terminal flutter, no pension physical—and I think I can guarantee that they'll listen."

"I see," Matthews said evenly.

"I have a theory, Tom," Stuarti said, righting himself on the bed with effort, "and it's this. That the ability to repress one's emotions—to bear the moral isolation—is a capital sum, and thus depleted by expenditure. Yours is gone, dear boy. Besides, I need *someone* to blame if I don't want to wind up in front of some irritated congressional oversight committee, and if all that protection costs is the career of some burned-out security guy, well, as the National Association of Manufacturers says, there's no free lunch. You're it," he beamed, raising the ginger ale in a toast, "and you're out. Cheers."

"You don't need any such thing," Matthews said, his eyes fond. "Whatever you had Kate hand him could just as easily have been delivered at the gate by commercial messenger."

"Better safe than sorry," Stuarti said brightly, then frowned. "Damn, start quoting the National Association of Manufacturers and you start *talking* like one."

For a long moment Matthews did not speak. When at last he did, his voice was shaky and his eyes were blinking rapidly.

"Mary . . ." he began.

"That's capitalism for you," Stuarti said quickly. "No job security anywhere. Nothing to be done about it, I'm afraid. Modern world."

Matthews smiled gratefully, and when he spoke his voice was again in control.

"Did you get the Bunny loaded?" he asked.

"Right to the tips of his long floppy ears," Stuarti said flatly, lowering his legs gingerly to the floor and reaching for his crutches.

"How bad is it going to be?" Matthews asked.

"That's an interesting question," Stuarti said. "In fact, it's the same one that Blaine keeps asking me. Every half hour or so. And then makes these melodramatic throwing-up noises when I tell him the truth. Which is, I don't know.

"Everyone understands treason in war," Stuarti continued, almost to himself. "It's clear and it's simple. But the sort of threat that Bunny represents is subtler, and more profound in its consequences. A society of liberal institutions, such as ours, requires more *trust* from people than any other. Consent and promises are the sole ties of our constitutional vision. Subversion is a betrayal not only of constitutional government and of the people, but of the system of trust itself. We *all* know that, for Christ's sake!

"How ambitious is Bunny?" Stuarti asked. "Will he be willing, on the basis of unexamined evidence, to make the country look bad in order to make himself look good? I don't know, but I *think* so. He's known, at least since the death of Butterfield, that Berg's a baddy, and it didn't slow him down. I'm inclined to regard that as the crossing of a moral Rubicon. But *will* he speak? For *sure*?" Stuarti shrugged. "Tune in next week. If he does, I'm afraid that he's likely to embarrass himself. But then that's better than getting your head blown off when you answer the phone, so I don't think I'm going to worry about that too much. Who knows? Maybe he's got a good sense of humor."

Again they looked at one another in silence, Matthews's eyes newly calm beneath the caterpillar of sutures, Stuarti's face somehow swollen, as though congested with unsobbed sobs.

"Kate's outside," Stuarti said finally.

Matthews nodded.

"She's a fine woman, Tom," Stuarti said, and now it was his voice that was not wholly in control.

Matthews nodded again. "What about you, Mary?" he asked.

"Frank's got a condo down in Boca Raton," Stuarti said.

"He's invited me down week after next. Thinks I should take a firsthand look at Retirementland."

"You won't make it," Matthews said, smiling. "The arthritis'll provide short-term cover, but you're nowhere *near* old enough to run it for long."

"Why, thank you, dear boy," Stuarti said, and when he stood his eyes were shining. "Thank you very much."

Then Kate was somehow in Matthews's arms, weeping and saying his name, and when at last he again raised his eyes to the doorway Stuarti was gone.

CHAPTER TWENTY-FOUR

THOUGH the source of the leaks was never determined, the rumors in the press corps began the next day.

A spy had been caught, said some with confidence; a press conference was imminent. A spy had escaped, others whispered; state secrets had gone awry. The *Washington Post* was more specific, identifying the secrets vaguely as nuclear, and a syndicated columnist at the Press Club spoke with knowing sorrow of impending strains within the Atlantic Alliance.

Thus diffuse on the Friday, the rumors—each hour spreading globally courtesy of Mr. Bell's entertaining invention—gathered force and focus over the next thirty-six hours, coming at last to consensus on the locus, if not the substance, of the breaking story.

Thus it was that the international media, seized with that feeding frenzy provoked only by the scent of unknown blood, foregathered that Sunday in London's Hyde Park, where that afternoon a rally would be held under the sponsorship of the Campaign for Nuclear Disarmament, and all uncertainty drowned in a deluge of ink.

*　*　*

The day was radiant, and the organizers of the rally claimed a crowd of 200,000, a figure that the police did not dispute.

Though the realities to be addressed were grim, there was a decidedly festive air to the gathering. Cardboard missiles and caricatures of international leaders danced above the throng on poles, like Chinese dragons. Clowns, jugglers, and mimes performed, and a group of affectless Japanese dressed in sack-cloth passed out graphic photos of the victims of Hiroshima and Nagasaki, much to the irritation of the food vendors.

The opening speaker set the afternoon's tone.

If our governments do not want war, she demanded simply, why do they spend all this money on weapons?

Could it be mere coincidence, she asked more darkly, that while millions of pounds are spent on arms, millions of people are starving?

To these unanswerable questions—or, at least, unanswered ones—the throng responded with a single voice.

Small and brave, she stood alone above them, waiting until outrage was spent and the crowd again was still.

It was her privilege that afternoon, she said, to introduce an American, to which the crowd, surprisingly, responded with cheers, as though to affirm that solidarity with life knew no national boundaries or merely parochial prejudice.

An American, she continued, who, until forty-eight hours ago, had been employed as a "senior expert" by the United States Arms Control and Disarmament Agency, to which the crowd response was understandably mixed; hoots for experts, governments, and bureaucratic entities, cheers for disarmament and forty-eight hours of moral health.

An American, she concluded simply, who at incalculable risk to his family, his career, and even his life itself, would that day bring confirmation of their grimmest fears, and thus new urgency to their crusade, an introduction not wholly hyperbolic, for while Bunny was single and in blooming health,

208

there would shortly be no doubt at all that his career was shot.

Given the time that he had had to prepare, Bunny's speech was masterful.

He spoke soberly of "the extinction of the species," the "death of death," and of "the corpse of mankind offered up on the altar of militarism."

It was not as an American citizen, he said, but rather as a citizen of the world, and with heavy heart, that he brought that day news of the most alarming nature.

And then he spilled the beans.

Less than seventy-two hours ago, he announced into the stillness, he had been present at a meeting of the president's Senior Arms Control Policy Group, at which the abandonment of arms control in favor of an open-ended arms race, the development of "dirty" nuclear weapons, and the deliberate targeting of civilian population centers had been codified in a National Security Decision Directive as the nation's policy.

He would not name names, he said—for any preoccupation with the merely *ad hominem* would only dangerously darken counsel—nor did he wish to impugn the motives of the madmen in question. He did not, he said, even ask to be thus easily believed.

He wished only, he said, that his voice be heard, and that the highly classified documents that he had obtained at that meeting be made part of the public record, to which end, though he could not permit them to leave his sight, the documents would be made available, for authentication and dissemination, to a select panel of archival experts under the joint auspices of *The Times* of London, *Le Monde*, and the International Institute for Strategic Study.

In closing, he once again emphasized his regret and his reticence, and declared that he would not have thus thrust himself forward had he not perceived it as his moral obligation "to choose between the nuclear race and the human race."

The crowd awarded him both ears and the tail.

The rally concluded with a four-minute "die-in," the vast throng sprawled in solemn silence as the media representatives flapped phoneward like carrion birds.

The time difference between London and New York permitted the film of Bunny's speech to be shown that evening on the network news.

Though Kate and Matthews were gardening together—building a trellis for the Romano pole beans—and thus did not see the news, Stuarti, watching in New York over Bullard's coq au vin, delightedly declared the footage to be the finest that he had seen since John F. Kennedy, in default of a speechwriter sufficiently fluent in German to know that a "berliner" was idiomatic parlance for a common breakfast bun, had stood defiantly before the Wall and stirringly declared, "I am a doughnut!"

European response to Bunny's disclosures was predictably fevered. "Cri de Coeur!," bannered *Le Matin*; "Pentagon Papers II," read the headline in the *Guardian*. Rotterdam's *NRC Handelsblad* declared openly that the time for a reevaluation of the NATO command structure had arrived, and even the pro-alliance *Neue Zürcher Zeitung* could ask only that its readers await the American response.

Alas, no official American response was forthcoming, and the White House spokesman, with some irritation, declared flatly that there would be none. Official restraint, in fact, was very nearly total, so that an interview with the secretary of defense, scheduled three weeks previously with the editors of Munich's *Süddeutsche Zeitung* and conducted in the hours preceding the imposition of institutional silence, received considerable play.

Confronted unexpectedly with Bunny's charges (indeed, how

210

could it have been otherwise?), the secretary, it was reported, actually laughed aloud. The American position on reduction of nuclear weapons? Devoutly to be wished, he said, observing mildly that Soviet expansionism, not disagreement over arms control, seemed to him the main problem in East-West relations. Queried about a deliberate policy of escalation, the secretary smilingly offered as analogy the dollar-auction game devised by Dr. Martin Shubik of Yale University.

The game, he explained, went as follows. Auction a dollar bill, but make it an odd auction in which the highest bidder buys the dollar for whatever he bid, but the second-highest bidder has to hand over whatever he bid as well, with no dollar in return.

Once two players have carried the bidding, in dimes, to $1.00 against 90 cents, he continued, the 90-cents bidder is forced to choose between bidding $1.10 for the dollar—a patent irrationality—or paying 90 cents for nothing. Typically, he said, as Dr. Shubik's research had shown, he chooses to raise the bid.

The dollar-auction game, the secretary pointed out, had much in common with an arms race. Once ensnared, the bidders quickly reach a point where higher bids add to their potential losses without increasing their chances of winning. Similarly, in an arms race, both sides spend ever-increasing amounts of money without improving their strength relative to each other. Such an arms race, he observed, could only and ever be an exercise in futility, adding, with a twinkle, that we had not become the nation that we were by paying a buck-ten for a dollar.

The secretary's interview was widely granted the status of a bravura performance, and if, to those familiar with his more normal rhetorical range, the reference to current research in game theory seemed perhaps a trifle tony, well, it was a risk that Stuarti had decided worth running when he wrote the script.

211

On Tuesday morning the documents were declared to be forgeries.

Though the full report of the archival experts was daunting in its complexity, the summary stated, without equivocation, that while the cover sheets (indicating level of classification) appeared genuine, the xerography paper was unquestionably Czech in provenance, and the type face used in the draft NSDD bore anomalies unique to a font of East German manufacture.

At a hastily called news conference at the offices of the Campaign for Nuclear Disarmament—where, having been granted "humanitarian sanctuary" and provided with a *garde de corps* consisting of an Anglican prelate, a spokesperson for animal rights, and six members of a radical ecology group—Bunny harshly accused his British hosts of collusion with the United States, and vilified the archival experts as "dupes of the CIA." His earlier reticence to name names also evaporated in the heat of the moment; those in attendance at the warmongering meeting of the Sackpig were listed by name and rank, including, though not limited to, the secretary of defense, two members of the Joint Chiefs of Staff, the deputy national security advisor, and the assistant secretary of defense for international security policy.

These intemperate remarks were poorly received.

British public opinion was representatively expressed by *The Economist*, which wrote icily that "collusion with the United States, under the name 'alliance,' has a rather long, and not wholly shameful, institutional history," and *Le Monde*'s representative to the archival board, incensed beyond bearing at being "traité d'un 'dupe' Americain," spoke frankly of Bunny as an "escroc," which was variously translated in the Anglophone press as "crook" or "fraud."

Once again there was no formal American rebuttal, and thus it fell to the media—benefiting both from the time lag and from unusually rapid and successful research—to report that evening, in voluminous detail, that on the day and date cited by Bunny as that of the SACPG meeting, the assistant secretary of defense for policy had been, as he was still, in Seoul, Korea, the deputy national security advisor in London, the Air Force chief of staff at Grumman Aircraft on Long Island, and the chief of naval operations in bed at Bethesda Naval Hospital with the gout.

Indeed, of the principals cited in attendance by Bunny, only the secretary of defense had even *been* in Washington the previous Thursday, and it was a generously documented matter of public record that he had, that day, hosted at the Pentagon a luncheon for seventy-five.

In all, the day was a poor one for Bunny's credibility, creating uncertainty in the minds of even those most sympathetic to his cause.

Mercifully, the uncertainty only endured for eighteen hours.

The next morning Kate and Matthews had the children of Kate's cottage to a picnic lunch. The sutures above Matthews's left eye were due to be removed that day, and after lunch, in a delicate operation with nail scissors and tweezers (Kate operating, Herbert Bevis assisting), they were snipped and pulled free, a procedure that came to crisis in the moment when Matthews actually said "Ouch!," triggering a paroxysm of sympathetic weeping alleviated only by adjournment to the recovery room and the oral administration of toll house cookies all around.

Thus it was that they missed the noon news conference, carried live by all three networks and PBS, conducted in New York by Senior Special Agent Francis Minihan of the FBI.

The news conference began with the announcement, after an investigation of long standing, of the arrest on espionage charges of two Soviet operatives, given as a Yuri N. Korolev and a Marya Dimitriovna Berg, and of the concomitant application, on similar charges, for warrants of extradition in Bunny's regard.

In a bureaucratic voice of leaden finality, which in its very

213

restraint seemed somehow to preclude the possibility of error or appeal, Minihan presented a detailed and sequential history of Bunny's perfidy, from his recruitment to his final and factitious betrayal.

Where it was deemed helpful, photo exhibits were introduced: Berg and Korolev together on the corner of Fifty-eighth Street, Berg and Bunny doing the Dance of the Documents at the Central Park seal pond, the bodies of Butterfield and the two innocent girls, and, in a sequence reminiscent of a cautionary tale, the photos of Andreas as an up-and-comer on the front page of the Cuban party paper and as a corpse on the floor of the East Sixth Street charnel house.

Most extraordinary of all, it was widely agreed, was the live testimony of the Berg woman, who, after tearfully stating that she preferred to throw herself on the mercy of an American court rather than return, a failure, to the Soviet Union, not only corroborated the broad outline of the Bureau's charges, but also provided, reading from notes, those details of Bunny's payment and maintenance that could only have been known to a case officer, even to deposit dates and foreign account numbers, the confirmation of which, in the days that followed, by then surprised no one.

The next morning a CND spokesperson shamefacedly announced that Bunny had gone missing, and for those involved with the case, fearing suicide, the hours that followed were difficult.

Stuarti, wheeled protesting to the park by Bullard for the sun, was rude about Bullard's new sports coat, observing that "with an ass like yours, double vents make you look like a giant thrush."

Minihan, morosely accompanying them, drank.

Kate and Matthews gardened relentlessly, weeding and thinning until dark, and in the evening built sprouting flats from scrap lumber; these in the spring they would fill with milled sphagnum and vermiculite, which a radiant Mrs. Mulready assured them to be superior to potting soil.

Thus when on that Friday afternoon (EST), Bunny appeared at the Stockholm airport, briefly vilifying the West and its media in an interview with *Dagens Nyheter* before departing for the East and a welcome whose details were unavailable, there was a collective moment of relief and a small, intensely drunken, cast party.

Kate and Matthews received that evening a lavish bouquet of flowers, which the local florist, in the absence of a card, could only tell them had been paid for in New York, and it was in fact that evening that they conceived a child, contrary to their convictions of each evening prior.

Stuarti's postcard arrived ten days later, bearing a Glo-in-the-Dark painting of the Eiffel Tower and a postmark from the Seventh Arrondissement:

> Obliged to leave F. in Boca Raton. Sun excellent for hips, but place v. depressing as sprightly and senile crumblers *partout*. Can be reached at the Montalembert for next four weeks as apt. requires painting. Trust Blaine can explain to GAO. Tante bella cose, etc.,
>
> S.
>
> P.S. Why would anybody name a town Rat Mouth?

215